Critical Acclaim for
JANE RANSOM and *BYE-BYE*

"Ransom's novel is both mind-boggling and alarming. *BYE-BYE* is *Basic Instinct* in book form. If you liked Sharon Stone in the movie, you'll love Ransom's protagonist, Rose Anne Waldin. . . . By far the most intriguing novel written that arouses all divisions and varieties of psychology as well as indulging philosophical ideologies."

—*West Coast Review of Books*

"The sex scenes, handled unapologetically and without coyness, are vivid and fresh."

—*Publishers Weekly*

"The most exciting book of its kind to come along in years. And just what is its kind? That of the quest for truth—truth as immediate reality, rather than as a relic to be stashed in a savings account. The quest is pursued through the intertwining tangles of love, bisexual eroticism, and perhaps friendship."

—Harry Matthews,
author of *The Journalist* and *Singular Pleasures*

"Reading *BYE-BYE,* I felt driven by the desire to see what would happen next. The protagonist explores some mighty perturbing situations but ultimately, this is a book about 'self' and also, more subtly, about bravery, for to view oneself as honestly as his character does requires nothing short of courage."

—Lucy Grealy,
author of *Autobiography of a Face*

"Jane Ransom is gifted with a sharp eye for telling detail, a keen ear for the twists and turns of colloquial speech, and a wicked wit."

—Frederick Morgan,
editor of *The Hudson Review*

Also by Jane Ransom

Without Asking, Story Line Press (poetry)
Scene of the Crime, Story Line Press (poetry)

BYE-BYE

JANE RANSOM

WASHINGTON SQUARE PRESS
PUBLISHED BY POCKET BOOKS

New York London Toronto Sydney Tokyo Singapore

A Washington Square Press Publication of
POCKET BOOKS, a division of Simon & Schuster Inc.
1230 Avenue of the Americas, New York, NY 10020

Copyright © 1997 by New York University
Published by arrangement with New York University and
Jane Ransom

ISBN: 0-671-02708-5

First Washington Square Press trade paperback printing January 1999

10 9 8 7 6 5 4 3 2 1

WASHINGTON SQUARE PRESS and colophon are
registered trademarks of Simon & Schuster Inc.

Cover design and illustration by Bascove

Printed in the U.S.A.

New York University Press gratefully acknowledges the support of Madeline and Kevin Brine in making these awards possible.

The New York University Press Prizes for Fiction and Poetry

In 1990, New York University Press launched the Bobst Awards for Emerging Writers to support innovative, experimental, and important fiction and poetry. As the prestige of the awards has expanded in recent years, so too has their mandate. The awards were originally conceived to publish authors whose work had not yet appeared in book form. We now include authors who, while often already a known quantity, remain unrecognized relative to the quality and ambition of their writing.

We have thus renamed the awards the New York University Press Prize for Fiction and the New York University Press Prize for Poetry. In 1996, the jurors selected Jane Ransom's novel, *Bye-Bye,* and Anne Caston's collection of poems, *Flying Out with the Wounded.*

For M.M.

ACKNOWLEDGMENTS

Thanks to Amy Pierpont and Nancy Miller for so pleas-antly welcoming me to Pocket Books. The biggest thank-you, regarding this paperback edition, must go to my agent, Charlotte Gusay, whose awe-inspiring determination and high professionalism are complemented by the fact she's fun to have a drink with.

I offer my sincere gratitude for encouragement and inspi-ration to Barbara Sang, Tsipi Keller, Tom Pappas, Linda Chester, Mary Burt, and Bob Covington, and particular thanks for brilliant editing to Barbara Epler, and for insight-ful criticism to Laurie Fox, Michael Mandler, Dorothea Stillman Halliday, and the indefatigable Andrew Kaufman.

Thanks also to *Lingo: A Journal for the Arts* for first publish-ing an excerpt of this book.

BYE-BYE

I draw her outline, head to toe.

What follows is not easy.

I pin the bottom of the page under my right wrist, while tugging the top margin up with my left hand, stretching the paper taut like the side of a pup tent. With my right hand I stab the picture repeatedly with a needle, staying inside the lines, never pricking the same place twice.

Now her skin's as rough as a cheese grater. I clip around the riddled figure, wad her into a crisp sponge, drop her into hot chocolate.

Bye Mom.

My mother used to stride through country fields trailing her palms along the weed tops, unleashing clouds of insects. While I chew patiently, cowlike, the paper dissolves into many bits. I think of the way she sucked on stalks of grass. Yummy, chocolate. How she spit on dry stones to make them shine.

A real flirt.

She habitually caressed her coffee spoon while she talked, slipping her thumb into and over its curves, along its edges, around and around and around, without looking. I had to look, mesmerized, mute. I swallow hard to get it down, gritty chocolate cement coating my tongue.

My mother was hard to get rid of. Because in fact she was already gone. How do you throw out a tenant who left yesterday? How do you evict a ghost? Alive or dead, my mother has always haunted me. Although I spent relatively little time with her, I could never get out from under her.

"No, dear. *Orson* Welles did the radio broadcast, but *Herbert George* Wells wrote the book."

As she spoke, my mother patted the inside of my elbow to comfort me in my stupidity. We sat thigh to thigh, having steak at the Ponderosa because Mom was visiting me at college, a very rare visit. My boyfriend gazed back and forth, waiting.

"Is that right?" he finally said for me, looking at her. "Wells, wells, wells."

She smiled, bravo, winked at him, squeezing my arm.

Whether it was *The War of the Worlds* or the world's wars, I could never compete. She always outdid me. She always knew better.

"Exactly what do you mean by that, dear?"

"Oh it's just, like, a phrase, Mom. You know."

She didn't trust me, not even after my graduation in journalism, magna cum laude. Without warning I had dropped by California to see her.

"Well let's think." Mom didn't give up. "There's really no such thing as 'just a phrase.' When you say, as you did just now, 'Occupying Grenada isn't exactly the Normandy conquest,' one wonders just *which* Normandy conquest you're referring to."

"I meant the famous one." Now I was in trouble. Mom had caught me.

"The famous one! Really dear, let's think. The 'Norman Conquest' came when William the Conqueror invaded England in 1066, whereas the 'Normandy campaign' refers to the Allied invasion of the Continent in 1944. These are both famous, but neither's precisely 'the Normandy conquest.' You see your mistake."

I wanted to be as ruthlessly intelligent as she was.

That was my mistake. We had the same name for a while, sure, but we'd never be equals.

I could never catch up. She had been menstruating for years and years by the time I got my period in fifth grade. I still love the smell of new Kotex. I don't know why. Sometimes dogs go crazy over shoes, sniffing the leather like drug addicts. That same year my breasts grew big as hers. She forbade me to wear a bra. "You're too young. And because I said so." The boys tortured me at recess, calling me "Jiggle Tits," "Floppy Knockers," and "Boom Boom Bazoom." But Mom did invite me to try tampons. "Here, let me put it in for you." I wanted to say no, but I couldn't say anything.

I wondered about her motives.

Why she left us the following year. Women are tricky like that. They pretend to be your mother then poof, they're gone. Surely, it was her departure that eventually gave me the courage to finish her off. Still, I think we loved each other. If ever I do get another dog, I'll name it after her. "Sit, Mom. Heel, Mom. Stay, Mom. Play dead, Mom. Good Mom. Bad Mom. Bad, bad Mom." She's actually dead, not playing. "Good girl!" And I'm . . . *smart* now. Got it? There are plenty of other women around if I want that kind of company. I'm not under anybody's thumb, not anymore, not unless I want to be.

•   •   •

I yawn wide as a horse and try to remember if whoever's beside me is male or female. I slide my hand along the ceiling of the blanket suspended between us, take blind aim, lower my hand. An erection. Large, firm . . . cold. Some lesbian with a strap-on dildo? Wait. I feel balls. Also cold. A strap-on with balls attached. I drop my hand farther, to stroke the inside of the thighs . . . *cold*. I open my mouth to scream, then don't. Although now I realize that even if I wanted to, I could not wake this man, now or ever—nevertheless, I disengage myself from the sheets as stealthily as possible.

"Get up."

My Lover has once again rudely awakened me.

"I said, get up. You're so helpless like this in the morning. Anyone could do what they want with you. *Get up*. Darling, would you make me breakfast?"

"Some dead guy was in bed with me."

"Better dead than alive," she says. "Dead men have fabulous hard-ons."

"Did you tell me that last night?"

"I'll tell you that every night if it makes you happy. Anything for your pleasure. Only please make me breakfast. *Us*. Make *us* breakfast."

"Yeah. Some dream. Gotta pee first—"

"Don't forget to uh, wait a minute, I didn't get a chance last night, untie your uh, from the—"

"*Ow*. Fuck. Just fucking untie me *now*."

"I guess," My Lover says. "Although you do look

nice, all twisted up on the floor. A little bruise would spice up that knee anyway."

"Fuck you."

. . .

But the truth is, *bruises* don't bother me. They are social butterflies, making colorful appearances, without depth. They don't hurt. For menstrual cramps, I bite my hand, to shift the pain around, get it confused. Like most perversions, this is not very original.

One of the best experiences I've ever had was waking up from an abortion. I found myself floating in an astonishing absence of discomfort or anxiety. It was Demerol. It didn't last. What I can't figure out is whether anesthetics *eliminate* or merely *conceal* suffering. Does the pain still exist even if you don't feel it? This is like that Zen koan about the falling tree. Puzzles and anesthetics give me pleasure, opening a trap door in my claustrophobic self-consciousness.

My Lover is a puzzle. My Lover is an anesthetic. My Lover is a religion—a vague, impersonal power, pleasant to surrender to. Sometimes it's healthy to go to a doctor who touches you all over, then addresses you with no more warmth than an IRS agent. I imagine men pay prostitutes for this kind of distant intimacy. Women can get it free from each other, hug kiss hug kiss, *chérie.*

My Lover is the opposite of my ex-husband, in gender and in relation to me. With him, I was always feeling something. Marriage riddled me with emotion, slow rages that wrecked my posture for days, greedy joys that threatened to catapult me into the fourth dimension, or even into having kids. When I myself was a kid, our family dog licked and licked my new kitten until the kitten was dizzy with happiness. Mommy, Mommy. Well I assumed it was happiness.

Back home after the operation, my husband served me dinner in bed: spinach pie and a Middle Eastern lamb stew he had made, following his family recipe. I've rarely felt so taken care of. Hubby, hubby. He resembled Mom more than she herself ever did. My mother was not the nurturing type. But she and my husband were both the stoic, strong-minded, attractive, overall superior type. Which explains how I finally won her attention by having won his.

Back then, I lived in the real world. I remember it well. We had been married quite a while. I had grown used to my husband's physical proximity and my mother's distant brilliance. And then *Shazam!* my mother was suddenly there beside me, flesh and blood, while my husband's image flickered across the TV sky. *She* had arrived in New York the same evening *he* spent in Washington being interviewed on CBS.

It was the first time I had seen my mother in years. It was the first time she had seen my husband, ever. There he was explaining on air some plan to replace the franc, the mark, the pound, and the peso with a single European currency. Mom was ecstatic:

"So attractive. So well informed. So articulate."

That was just like my mother.

I was more cautious, remembering Esperanto and the metric system. But my husband said: "This can work. Money is whatever the various governments say it is, and people have to use it. Don't they."

Mom raised her index finger and nodded at the TV: "Absolutely."

After that she embraced him as her own. This began the next day when they met in person. "What a superb interview. . . . You have such a fine grasp of European politics. And you put forth your points so elegantly. Money is a fascinating topic, much more complicated than most people realize."

That was just like my mother.

My husband nodded and thanked her politely, then turned to throw his arms around me, saying, "Sweetheart, Sweetheart. I missed you." Mom eyed me up and down as if meeting *me* for the first time. It was the beginning of a new era. She glanced at him again, as if to make sure. But it was clear: he would never betray me.

Things seemed simpler back then, when I lived in the real world. But whether they actually were or not, I can't tell. It did *seem* as if my life were following one reasonable thread—which since then has frayed into many strands, raveling and unraveling beyond control.

When I bought the first oil painting, it felt slightly more eccentric than ordering a slogan T-shirt like the one my brother sent away for, that says, "I AM GOD." I didn't like the painting, but that had nothing to do with it. I was curious. Curiosity is a dangerous drive. Oh, kitty, kitty.

But as the paintings began to stack up, I did start to suspect myself of some hidden motive. I now wonder if that's redundant. Probably all my true motives are hidden (or at least misplaced). So many things are redundant, repetitious, copies of copies, ad infinitum. In any case, I was more concerned with what people would think. I didn't hang the pictures for fear someone would see them and assume I was losing my mind. People began to suspect me of that, after the divorce.

I have the paintings on my walls now. They're pure kitsch, disturbing and tacky, but I'm drawn to them. Most women are fascinated by murder and mayhem. My husband—ex-husband—once told me that in some parts of the world, women can be put to death for wanton behavior like mine, and—But there I go, raveling.

• • •

"Here we are: over easy, toast, jam, bacon, juice, coffee."

Why does My Lover always want me to cook for her?

And how is it that my ex-husband, such a busy man, can shop for and prepare perfect meals four or five nights a week, and not have a nervous breakdown? Whereas it sometimes takes me days to garner the specific energy to fetch groceries. Flaunting her financial superiority, My Lover has all her groceries delivered from Dean & Delucca.

She doesn't know about the paintings.

My Lover photographs women with women. She is somewhat notorious within the small world of lesbian pornography. (As a teenager, I myself used to draw little pictures; sometimes they were of a woman and a man, but sometimes they were just of a woman, with legs open.) Many magazines pay My Lover well for her work, although some don't. An article about her first caught my attention two years ago, in *On Our Backs*. The article was accompanied by a self-portrait boasting biceps and crewcut. I looked up her number in the Manhattan White Pages.

"Hello," I said. "I just wanted to say I'm a great admirer of your art."

She did not thank me because she did not believe me. She asked me my age and name, in that order. She told me she was having a dinner party that night and that I was welcome to prepare the meal. I agreed immediately. I put on my black suede shorts whose zipper ran in a U shape—from my bellybutton, down under my crotch, and back up to the top of my buttocks between my two dimples. (I owned a few interesting outfits even then. Divorce does that.)

I arrived with groceries at 5:30. Meeting her in person, I felt annoyed. It was going to be my first time with a woman; I had thought it would be better if she looked like a man. But in real life she turned out to be girlishly petite, much smaller than the photo had suggested, and also much prettier—with her Judy Davis lips and wide, intelligent forehead.

"My guests will be here in two hours," she said. I prepared babaganoush, cucumber and yogurt salad, basmati rice with caramelized onions, green beans with garlic, and the lamb, braised in cumin, coriander, and cinnamon; my ex-husband had taught me to cook. While I worked, she talked. "Are you sure that's going to be ready on time? That stuff in the bowl looks greasy. Not everybody likes garlic. My God, don't overdo it with the salt there."

The guests were eight women, all except one over forty. The exception was a twenty-three-year-old former Miss Kansas. All the guests, including Miss Kansas, approached me (or rather, distanced themselves from me) with condescension, pity, and glee. I was immediately recognized as one more bimbo in a long line of My Lover's bimbos. Intuitively I acted the part, smiling dumbly, dashing about with trays and decanters, giggling inappropriately, wildly bobbing my head to mean "yes" or even "maybe." Later on, after the other guests had gone, I received high rewards for my efforts, once my host finally felt compelled to test the zipper on my shorts.

(It worked.)

•   •   •

Dear _____,

Each time I think I'm safely on the way, suddenly I find myself sliding back into nostalgia, memories of us together, our marriage, how happy we were together before the crisis hit. Or at least, how happy I REMEMBER us being. Because I've begun to suspect we were never really happy, but perhaps that possibility is too devastating to consider. Because if we weren't happy, if we were only pretending to be happy, what exactly were we, really?

But I know you hate it when my mind begins to work this way—both you and my mother were always much clearer thinkers than I ever was—so I'll try to get to the point. Actually I think that you and my mother were always much too similar, but again, that is not the point.

You've made it clear that our divorce is final—of course I have to agree with you—and yet, in many small ways, it seems you can't resist leading me on, you can't resist being just forgiving enough, just cruel enough, just attentive enough, to keep me tied to you.

That all my friends became your friends compounds my difficulties: since our divorce you have made sure to keep in touch with them—so that even when I just want to relax with an old friend, I cannot get away from you. It has reached the point, in fact, where now I need to get away from all those old friends as well. The past, our past, threatens to suffocate any new life I make for myself.

Why I've let this happen, why I've been helpless to rid myself of this situation, why I've allowed myself to remain in the torture chamber of a dead love, is a bottomless mystery to me—but that's how it is. Therefore, I have decided to disappear. You've probably figured out I didn't go to Paris. There's room in New York for both of us now. I'll call you later, maybe in a few years.

•   •   •

I've mentioned how I first met My Lover after seeing her in a *magazine*. But those can be unreliable, and I generally prefer to learn from *books,* especially library books, which carry institutional authority. A year ago (a year after meeting My Lover), I made a copy of my birth certificate; this was the step which *several library books* suggested come first. Next, I whited out my name on the birth-certificate copy, and in its place put another: *Rose Anne Waldin.* Then I made a copy of that copy. I stamped this second copy with a "Certified" stamp, scribbled on the line where a notary public's signature was supposed to be, and embossed over the stamp with a "Certified" embossing seal. I had found the name *Anne Waldin* by blindly inserting my finger in the phone book. To make the name different I had added Rose, for *Rose Anne Waldin.* (I wanted to be *Rosie* because I never really have been.)

I bought a black, China-doll wig half as long as my own light-brown hair. I replaced my tortoise-shell glasses with contact lenses that made my brown eyes green. Wearing the wig and lenses, I used Rosie's birth certificate as an I.D. to get a driver's license. As Rosie, I parallel parked better than my old self ever had. A good start.

With Rosie's license and birth certificate in hand, I went next to the Social Security office (again, exactly as the library books suggested). Rosie explained that despite her thirty-five years, she had never acquired a Social Security number—her parents had been putting her through school all this time—but now she was employed and her new boss said she needed one. Soon she was 075–08–9713.

The following week, I liquidated some of my modest inheritance and had almost ten thousand dollars in money orders made out to Rosie. At that time I was living on the Lower East Side. I walked northwest to Chelsea, where I opened a Citibank account as Rosie. This went smoothly because I had the Social Security number and driver's license. After seeing the money orders, Citibank also gave Rosie a VISA card.

For the next two weeks, I looked for apartments in Chelsea. Again wearing the wig and the contact lenses, I went door to door, asking the superintendents about vacancies. Eventually I secured a sixth-floor one-bedroom. The previous tenant had left behind several pieces of cheap, raw-pine furniture. In my old life I would have perhaps finished it in some natural tone, or else trashed it, but now I painted it all pink, *rose pink*.

I did not want to move in one fell swoop from the old place to the new, because that could attract attention and create *witnesses* who might someday connect Rosie with my old self. This, I wanted to avoid. It was imperative that no one catch me at Rosie's place, or her at mine. I began visiting the Chelsea apartment regularly but furtively, donning the wig and doffing my old eyeglasses en route, and each time dropping off a few of my belongings. Within three months, I had transferred various utensils, dozens of books, my laptop, and my collection of oil paintings. I gave old furniture and clothes to the Salvation Army. (After all, I'm a kind person, a good person.)

As I prepared to finally move in, I began to fantasize that my husband would try to track me down. The more I fantasized about it, the more alluring the possibility became, however implausible. Fantasy often supplements my reality. At times in the past, when applying for employment, I first *fantasized* about the upcoming interview, in order to bolster my confidence.

Yes, fantasy's handy for managing fear. Today's woman is compelled to "fantasize" being taken by gunpoint to some underground chamber—but there I go.

The first thing that an intelligent stalker like my husband would look for would be a forwarding address. With that in mind, I informed my old post office that I was leaving for a remote part of China. "There will be no mail service where I'm going. Anything comes for me, just throw it away." The clerk nodded vaguely. Her bifocals were crooked. Sometimes postal workers snap suddenly. Without an address, I could no longer buy mail-order artwork, but maybe I'd had enough.

On the other hand, I did want to be able to receive some correspondence, in order to maintain business relations with my lawyer and my accountant, particularly in case Rosie got into trouble and I had to dump her in a hurry. So I sent my lawyer and my accountant a false-lead forwarding address, of a postal-box service in Chicago. I arranged it so that now the Chicago service secretly forwards my mail to another service in Cincinnati, which in turn forwards it to one in Detroit, which finally forwards it to New York. It ends up at Mail Mall, a safe six blocks away from PostWorld, where Rosie rents a box. All this subterfuge may have been unnecessary (my ex-husband would never stalk anyone) but it made me feel sought after, important, and in control.

Last April, I finished becoming Rosie. I dyed my hair bluish black, and had it cut like the wig. I put together a wardrobe of high heels and lots of vinyl and velour in the bright colors of the paintings. My earlier self had been mostly the beige-or-gray, linen-or-wool type. I wasn't planning to hurt anyone, but I did all at once feel as giddy as some teenager who kills both parents and burns down the house, later blaming it on ritual abuse. I also bought a waffle iron and began eating waffles with butter and syrup at least once a day. I miss my slim silhouette but make up for it with large doses of eyebrow pencil, liner, mascara, and lipstick.

Once I was moved in, I unwrapped the paintings and hung them in every room except the bedroom. I wanted to immerse myself in another's work. I exempted the bedroom only because I suffer from insomnia. The paintings are alarmingly simple, but they were done by *a famous man*. So far they have had little effect, that I can tell.

. . .

I used to own only one piece of original artwork, a monotype my husband gave me for our first anniversary. I kept it after the divorce despite my better judgment; sometimes, nostalgia overwhelms me. Rosie mailed the monotype back to him three months ago. Probably he threw it away.

I remember the day we bought it. Neither of us knew much about contemporary art back then (I have changed in many ways), but that day he took me to the Totem Gallery and told me to pick out whatever I wanted. "The Sumitomo Bank just commissioned this gallery to do their new Fifth Avenue lobby. They never make a bad investment," my husband said. Years later, I learned more about the Totem's ignoble reputation. But back then, I trusted my husband's judgment in nearly all matters.

The show of monotypes at the gallery that day—all by a young man who later made it into the Whitney Biennial—included at least one penis per picture. Some of the penises were attached to bodies but others hovered like streptobacilli amid gelatinous backgrounds.

"High-class pornography. Let's go somewhere else," my husband said.

"What? I didn't hear you," I lied. "These are so beautiful. I definitely want one."

In that brief exchange lay our entire future (or lack thereof), all our basic irreconcilable differences: his intolerance, my dishonesty, his penchant for labels, my appetite for deviance, his fear of illicit sexuality, my tendency to dismiss his feelings. At the time, we knew nothing of what lay ahead.

The monotype I chose depicted an anguished face above two penises crossed in an X, a modern variation of the classic skull-and-crossbones motif. I recall that on that day in the Totem Gallery, this picture hung beside the boomerang-shaped desk of the owner qua receptionist. She sat reading a magazine, with perfect posture, her hair (red like my mother's) lacquered into a perfect helmet. Her self-assurance and proximity set me on edge.

"The way it's painted, this face almost resembles a theater mask," I announced. "I'm from a theatrical family, rather well known actually, and I've been applying to graduate schools, to study these things, uh, so maybe I'll take that picture." I remember speaking loudly.

She disengaged herself from her magazine. "I see. Well, how . . . *interesting*. Not many of our clients pursue such an *anecdotal* response to a piece. Dear, might I ask, are you a *serious* buyer?"

I recall how her voice reminded me of my mother, back when I myself used to paint pictures for Mom: "Why thank you," she would say. "What an *interesting* . . . tree. Isn't it. A tree." It was my mother who, so long ago, taught me neatness and manners: "I hope that you've put away the crayons and the paint set and cleaned up after yourself. Pretty please?"

"Wrap up that monotype for me *immediately*."

"My dear." The red-haired woman tucked in her chin. "The Totem Gallery is not Macy's, or Sear's or whatever you're used to. We'll have to discuss the form of payment, first, and then I'll need your name and address. We keep track of all our artists' work." She went on for quite a while, as I recall, and ended her lecture saying, "When all these steps have been completed, I will be glad to have my assistant prepare the monotype for safe transport."

I had never made love to another woman. And yet I instinctively longed to slap the receptionist.

"He'll take care of it," I said.

Of course, my husband always took care of everything.

． ． ．

My husband threw me out three years ago. *Infidelity.* My husband traveled a lot. In setting monthly allowances, bankruptcy courts understand that the more one is used to having, the more one needs, to get by. This truism applies to nonfinancial matters as well. Whenever my virile husband was away for long periods, I felt compelled to seduce other men.

Now I am good at keeping secrets, but then I wasn't. One day I told him about some minor tryst. (That's redundant; they were all minor.) My husband agreed to consider remaining married to me provided I get help. But therapy backfired: the more I talked to the therapist about my sexual indiscretions, the more sexual and indiscreet I grew. My husband discovered this somehow. I accused him of having read my date book or journal, but he swore he had read only my face. *Whump.* Out we fell from our Edenic garden.

At one point we were almost allowed back in, but came up against that age-old barrier, *the condom.* Yes, we were both disappointed in how it happened.

After ordering me to move out, my husband left for a long business trip. During his absence I found a new apartment, packed, and moved, crying throughout. I left my new number and address on his kitchen table (which had been *our* kitchen table) and the day after he returned to Manhattan he phoned. "Could I have the pleasure of your company at dinner tomorrow, Sweetheart?" My husband had not phoned once during his business trip. I had determined that if he ever did deign to call, I would be too busy to see him.

"Of course. I'd love to have dinner with you, whenever you want."

We went to the Cupping Room, which is where we had enjoyed our first drink together, some ten years earlier, on the Fourth of July night we met, as strangers, by accident. That night so long ago, we had each sallied forth alone to watch the fireworks from Battery Park. We had both arrived too late to see anything besides the throngs of people who had gotten there first. He was standing behind me, pressed up against me in the anonymous crowd, when I heard him sigh, "This is demoralizing." I had then turned, seen his large eyes, cinnamon-colored skin, and black mustache, and said, "I'd be happy—no, more than happy, very very happy, to *re*moralize you." And so we had left Battery Park and gone to the Cupping Room.

A decade later, it seemed our life had come full circle. Here we were married, separated, and in the Cupping Room again. He told me about his business trip—"We pulled it off without a hitch, once the Labor Department cooperated"—and I told him about my new apartment:

"It's cute. It's adorable. The view's fantastic." Something was wrong.

After dinner, we walked to my new place arm in arm. "Very nice. A bit small," he observed. He turned on and off the gas stove. He flushed the toilet without using it. He acted proprietary, as if this would be a kind of second home for us; I felt my life wobble like a forkful of Jell-O still inches from my mouth. I poured cognac into two paper cups. We drank. We talked. We kissed, sitting on my new futon sofa-bed. Eventually, we pulled out the bed and paused for birth control. "Why is the bed squeaking so much?" he asked. "Do you think it's assembled correctly?"

"I don't know, Sweetie. Maybe it's hitting the baseboards," I said, squeezing foam into my diaphragm.

My husband leaned to investigate behind the bed frame. There was a long silence. Then he said, "How stupid of me. As usual, I thought things were simple. I should have known, with you."

"What's the matter?"

"See for yourself."

I had tried to remove all traces of recent debauchery before his visit. Of course I hadn't been celibate after moving into my new place, but I had tried to be careful. Before his return I had hidden the bong, painted over the cigarette and wine stains on the window sill, washed the sheets, thrown out the empty bottles, vacuumed the rug, and swept the floor. But now I looked—at a torn, empty, foil Trojan envelope stuck in the crack between the floor and baseboard.

During the ensuing months of silence (he refused to speak to me for some time), it began to seem more and more unfair to me that once I had moved out, my having lovers should be seen as betrayal. I had assumed marital separation meant *permission to sleep around*. But my husband had imagined I would spend his absence thinking everything over, realizing how much I missed and loved him, and vowing to change my slutty ways. To discover (and at such a poignant moment) that the predicted transformation had not occurred, made my husband feel that he'd been made a fool of. For which he has never forgiven me.

• • •

GF, fortyish, overly educated, seeks "dinner conversation" with equally (if possible) brainy broad, in hopes of friendship or possibly more (and if so, lucky you). I don't necessarily expect you to be as attractive as I am.   *#2858*

I called *Le Supplément*'s personal-ad response number, punched in extension 2858, and left a message I hoped the *overly educated Gay Female* would understand: "I'm as discriminating as you are. Phone my answering machine as to when and where." I gave Rosie's name and number. Some days later the phone rang, I waited, the machine clicked on, and the message was left. "Friday, July 7, eight o'clock, 310 Riverside Drive, apartment 13-A."

I try to breathe slowly, calmly, but as the door to 13-A opens, I go numb. I stand gaping, too self-conscious to take in much of what she looks like. We each extend a hand, but neither of us steps forward. She's taller than me, like my mother. I lean far toward her and fear I may topple over like a corpse into her arms. Instead, we shake hands.

Then she bows her head, says something courteous, and ushers me in. The ceiling is low. I see only a few windows, and they begin high off the ground, as in a dungeon. The furniture is bulky and awkward, expensive yet dismal. She continues her urbane hostess monologue, beckons me further into the dark living room and hands me a full wine glass. Her short blond hair stands on end, gelled into a shocked position. "The responses so far haven't thrilled me," she says, referring to her ad in *Le Supplément,* New York's newest ultrasmart weekly.

She leans back in her swivel armchair; my turn. I'm thrown off balance by the gloomy apartment and the emerging fact that she is extraordinarily attractive, with a long neck, delicate ears, luminous blue eyes, Nordic cheekbones. I feel silly and demoralized, sunk into the marshmallow sofa. Then I remember I'm Rosie. And I notice the woman's stiff posture, not exactly prudish, but somehow snobby. *Time's up.* I reposition myself on the edge of her couch, lift my glass in a unilateral toast, observe its blood-colored contents against the light, and begin pontificating about wine.

"So what I'm saying is that basically there was a consensus among the eighteenth-century bourgeoisie to match instead of clash—*red* meat went with *red* wine, and *white* meat went with *white* wine—a lot like getting a *blue* handbag to go with your *blue* shoes. This proved you weren't lower class. Of course the really rich people, the aristocrats, didn't give a flying fuck and went on drinking whatever they felt like."

Rosie's little speech causes Personal Ad to drop her cigarette, burning a hole in the wool rug. The spot smokes and stinks for a second before Personal Ad picks up the cigarette, and grinds the embers under her heel. Immediately she mentions the Catholic Church's use of wine and (shrewdly, inspired by the smoking rug) *incense.* Oh she too is clever. "Incense didn't enter the Church until the Middle Ages, you know. There's nothing particularly Christian about it. The ancient Greeks used it, and so did the Egyptians. Just another example of Catholicism incorporating whatever social customs necessary to preserve its *ne plus ultra.*"

"Oh yes, of course," I say. I don't, in fact, know what

she means, because I don't understand Latin; but I *am* able, from my years of newspaper reading, to make fun of the Catholic Church's updated Universal Catechism: ". . . I guess *spiritual* speculation was always a sin, but now it seems that buying into Florida real estate can also send you straight to hell—which is something I've always suspected."

She doesn't laugh, but wanly smiles, as if politely. Over the next few hours, she brings out plates of olives and cheese, and each time, as she passes near, I stare at her prominent cheekbones and big blue eyes. Eventually we move to the dining room, where she sets on the table a fish-shaped dish holding saffron rice, lobster claws, clams, and mussels. She lights candles. The fish-shaped dish and the candles strike me as suspiciously premeditated. Women are known to be secretive killers, poisoning people, smothering children with pillows, administering injections to the unconscious. *I'm getting drunk.* If I were going to kill someone else, I'd do it differently.

I have noticed most women my age don't drink much anymore; after thirty, it gets ugly. By the end of dinner, she and I have finished off two bottles of wine. I sense her liking and disliking my image: China-doll hair, red silk vest, and platform sandals. We return to the living room and start in on a third bottle.

She takes the chair again. I sink helplessly back into the sofa. The more I drink, the more questions she asks.

But she remains stone faced and fails to respond to my answers, except with more questions. I adhere to the truth as much as I can; it makes lying easier. Every now and then, in a tossed-off aside, she reveals devastating facts about herself—"My uncle began raping me when I was fourteen"—and then swiftly withdraws each time and snares me with another question. "How did you feel about your brother's illness?" "Why don't you finish graduate school?" "How did your father lose his job?" Unable to turn our mutual gaze back onto her, I'm helplessly swept along by the interrogation, trying to keep my answers logically connected, but instead being pulled like a kite into some space where finally I am floating, alone, yet not free.

"So, Rosie, you've moved around a lot in the last few years. Rather rootless, aren't you. Interesting . . ."

Interesting was always an insult, coming from my mother. Such smug put-downs devastated my brother. They may have been what did him in. No, impossible. My brother was always a hopeless case. As for my father, when my mother sicced that word *interesting* on him, he was caught between not believing her and wanting to believe her. For years, she had *not* found my father interesting *in any way whatsoever,* and yet she continued to use the term against him: *interesting.* It was her most casual, cruel form of dismissal.

{28}

"I haven't been able to yet, but what I want is to get close enough to somebody so that I can trust them," Personal Ad says. *No, no, no.* I grab the kite string and hand-over-hand haul myself down through the stratosphere until I can touch ground and back away from her. Safe. But she craftily coaxes me toward her again with a question about happiness. I buckle and talk of suicide, surprising both of us. "Isn't there anything that makes you happy?" she asks. I feel my face collapse from wine and eternal depression.

"The dinner was wonderful. That rice stuff. Really delicious. If only I didn't have to get up so early tomorrow for my dental appointment. This was so nice of you . . . I want to reciprocate soon although I'd rather not have you over, I mean I'd rather take you *out,* you know, to a nice restaurant. Because I'm a terrible cook and, well, I don't have much of a kitchen in my new apartment."

"Certainly Rosie, you can cook something."

"No, it wouldn't be any good, really . . . I don't have any pans, there are only two burners—"

"Get some pans."

"Oh. Yes, you're right. Of course, I like to cook for other women. Okay. Anyway, it was fun."

She kisses my cheek without touching it.

• • •

In the elevator down, I change my mind. By the time I reach my apartment I'm desolate. Why did she let me go? I reach for the saucepan and slam it against the refrigerator. Then the same with the cast-iron frying pan. Of course I have *pans*.

She could not have known that I wanted (didn't I?) her to take hold of me, lift me up, toss me onto her bed, pull my vest off without unbuttoning it, yank away my sandals and pants, then turn her full attention to me. I wanted her to zoom in on me the way she had in conversation, impersonal and brutally personal. I wanted her to pin me down, nailing me to the kite-frame cross but with my legs open, a willing sacrifice—helpless and pure as a martyr, but free as a heathen.

I had not, in the end, encouraged her. Because I knew that if I did stay, then at the crucial moment, the moment when I should completely give in to her, I'd be compelled to push her off, I'd get on top, I'd make love to her with a frenzied stubbornness she would be no match for . . .

So instead. Instead of detaining me, she opened the door. I backed out of it, spun around to push the elevator button, clumsily hit "up" instead of "down," turned to make a joke about that, saw her door already closed.

Although it was late, I took the subway and found

myself in a train car, surrounded by men. *Nothing happened, but it could have.*

As I undress, shower fog encloses me, and an intoxicating sensation takes hold that I have escaped terrible danger. I keep the water very hot and wash everywhere, even between my toes. Afterward, I don my cotton nightie printed with pink and yellow kittens. Perched on the edge of the bed, I fantasize straddling her face. I fantasize smothering her that way, while we both climax, her climax the stronger one, occurring through death. Mine the actual climax, occurring through fantasy. Later, I review the dinner conversation, assure myself I gave nothing away. I wake in the night and declare out loud, "*No.* I won't have her over." I switch on all the lights, then go sit in the living room to contemplate the paintings and mull over my options. These paintings were done by a famous man.

· · ·

"What would you like me to do to you now?" My Lover asks.

"Maybe the blindfold. And don't tie me up, but hold something that feels like a gun to my head."

"Handcuffs?"

"Yes. No. I'm sorry, I don't know. I don't want to answer any more questions. Couldn't you ju—"

"Perfect," she concludes. "You're infinitely more lovable when you can't talk. A blindfold will go well with that . . . There. I'd like to make you wait on all fours while I go out shopping. 'Stay.' I appreciate such things, but you're not a real masochist. You'd be dry by the time I got back. Turn over, Darling. Hands behind you. You remember my ice pick? The blunt end's boring, I'm tired of seeing it. This is going to hurt some, because I'm not putting it where you really want it. For that place I have something else up my sleeve, as they say, Darling, although *they* don't mean it literally."

For the last three-and-a-half months, My Lover has acted as if my dramatically altered appearance made no difference. *And she is the only witness.* After conceptualizing Rosie, but before turning into her, I told all my friends I was moving to Paris. Until then, I had deeply resented my friends and anyone else who had ever observed my knocking over a glass, tripping on a carpet edge, or saying something stupid: "Yeah, I had all Patti Smith's records, or at least some. I wish she'd make a comeback, she was cool. When? Well I mean, I knew that."

I had decided that Rosie would display more aplomb.

During my first month as Rosie, I began frequenting my old friends' neighborhoods. Although I avoided running into my ex-husband, I began actively pursuing these ex-friends, staking out their apartment buildings, waiting for them after work and stumbling against them in the street *accidentally*. I would watch them turn away without recognizing me. Then I would go home, masturbate, and think of myself as superhuman, in the Nietzschean sense. I fell into the habit of drinking a cup of hot chocolate after these quality times alone, to maintain the celebratory mood. After a while that didn't seem to be enough, so I would also have a brownie, or a carton of ice cream, or a slice of pizza, or a pizza. Eventually I had to stop, or become truly obese. I understood: like some cat that's abandoned along the road but instinctively finds its way home, my depression had rediscovered me and moved back in.

But at least I am rid of my friends. For these first few months as Rosie, my only intimate acquaintance has been My Lover. I cannot get away from her. I once observed a sparrow perched on the wrist of a martial-arts aikido master. Whenever the bird tried to press its feet against him in order to take off, the master lowered his wrist an infinitesimal amount, exactly counteracting the bird's pressure. I could not actually see the sparrow's struggle, but inferred it. For as long as the master wished, the poor bird remained stuck.

The inability to sever contact can be terrible.

Like some mesmerist Svengali, My Lover holds me captive by feigning indifference. But other than her, I have severed contacts; I am no longer social. When Rosie goes out at night, she goes alone. I used to regularly see shows at East Village theaters, but now I mostly stay home. I like reading about performances whether I've seen them or not. Sometimes I prefer the review to the real thing. I buy newspapers and clip articles that reflect my particular tastes. Today I saved this from *Le Supplément*:

Dear Readers,

Consider that for twenty-some years, artists with vaginas have been unfolding the new map of the old uni-verse. God is dead, and so is the Great Goddess, but the Other lives on like some insect surviving Armageddon.

Freedom's nothin' left to lose, and because post-Freudian men fear castration, women nowadays feel freer than men. Eve's getting even more than ever. Female self-panalysts confess their original scenes and primal sins, and society runs amuck.

A hot, slimy muck.

Well it's all been super, but Honey, aren't you starting to get glutted? We've had Annie Sprinkle showing off her cervix, Lea Delaria playing toss-the-buttplug, Carolee Schneemann having orgies with dead fish, Diamanda Galas doing Satanic mass, and on and on and on. Do we really need any more?

As any woman in her right mind or left brain says: Yes. More. Now. Please.

And thank you.

It debuted last night at La Mama.

It may be female, dear readers, but I just can't tell. During the show it polled the audience, who voted to call it a "she." So at least for now I hail her as another hot climax of America's double-X-led genderation.

She walked onstage in coveralls, her face shadowed by a sequined sombrero. Various items stuck out of her pockets or hung from a tool belt. A metal suitcase turned out to be full of the same kinda stuff. What kinda stuff?

You know that since the sixties, we've seen musicians who can make an electric guitar out of anything from an axe to a toothbrush. Well, this witch has turned everything from rolling pins to telephone receivers to parking meters into *vibrators*.

After demonstrating how these things work (most have off/on switches, but the phone starts shaking when you dial "0," and the salad spoon needs merely to be turned upside down), she invited eight audience members to come onstage and bring their folding chairs with them. She lined them up and proceeded to *hypnotize* them.

Yes, it was all the usual "you-will-fall-into-a-deep-sleep" and "you-will-obey-my-every-command" kinda thing. And it *really worked* kinda thing.

She put on the soundtrack to *The Wizard of Oz*, and told them that as long as the music lasted, they would be five years old again and were to "play nicely" together with the various toys.

Gee, the things kids can do with vibrators! And you thought putting marbles up your nose used to be exciting.

Finally, the music stopped at "If I Only Had a Brain" and the "kids" woke up to loud applause. As they wobbled offstage, the hypnotist waved and went up in the proverbial puff of smoke.

Ushers handed out a flyer as the audience left the theater. All it said was that the Andorgenie plans never to perform the same act twice, and that the Andorgenie's second show will be next month at the A-Bawl in a double billing with award-winning Chicano poet Juan Rescate. See you there.

.   .   .

Nearly six months have passed since my last boyfriend. He was a jazz pianist. After my divorce I began dating nonlawyer types—musicians, artists, actors . . . Partly to avoid being reminded of my ex-husband, and partly because my own interests were becoming more arty, more ambitious, perhaps less realistic . . . oh well. The jazz pianist grew despondent whenever he played fewer than three gigs a week. At those times, he preferred eating or arguing to having sex. *Men!* They often seem hopelessly predictable or perhaps the opposite, hopelessly unreliable.

But I would be afraid to sign off men completely, just as nowadays I would be afraid to sign off women completely. Either way would be like locking myself in a room with no windows or doors. I have sometimes found, however, that it's easier to meet new lovers — *men* especially — when I'm not trying to. So, while I'd like to get a new boyfriend, I won't try too hard. Flexibility is the key — windows and doors.

The disadvantage of an apartment door, as compared to a house door, is that there are no windows beside it to look into before you announce yourself. I knock. Personal Ad appears in a black silk robe with a cat in her arms. The cat precludes our kissing hello. I run two fingers over its forehead and under its chin, grazing Personal Ad's small breasts.

"Hello. You've acquired a cat."

"Mm-hmmm, how observant of you. Pleasure to see you again."

"Thank you . . . I mean, you too."

"Come in?"

"Thank you. You look good with her, she's very

pretty. I've always liked pets. Love that orange and black combo."

"It's a male. Wine?" offers Personal Ad.

"Please . . . Thank you."

"Do you always have to say thank you?" Personal Ad looks as though she just took a bath. Her hair is damp, her face flushed, without makeup. She adds, "It seems overly polite."

"No I don't, I'm not, I mean . . . "

I had promised myself not to return Personal Ad's calls. But then she failed to call. After three weeks passed I sent her a letter confessing that I desired to see her, but could not bring myself to cook. Some days later, she phoned, but said nothing about the letter. I was too embarrassed to ask her whether she had gotten it. She invited me to drop by her place some evening for a drink.

"Of course, I'd love to. Whenever you want."

Personal Ad had revealed little during our first meeting. She's an insurance adjustor. She has a doctorate in psychology. She is working on some book about herself, using her psychology degree, okay. Her uncle first raped her when she was fourteen. Already, that is much more than I wanted to know. What interests me now about Personal Ad is her failure to call me. It reminds me of my mother, who is dead, but also of my father and brother, who never call me either, of course. I would rather not think about them.

Personal Ad must have sensed I was lying about being unable to cook. Cooking is easy. She probably thinks I'm homophobic and couldn't stand to take responsibility for our second date. She has summed it all up to herself like that, and then invited me over out of mock pity, trying to make herself look big, and me look small. She's completely off track, if not off her rocker. It's not about responsibility; it's about *the paintings*. I can't let her see them.

And something else. Since my divorce three years ago, I've changed addresses four times and the same thing happens each time: Within a few months, my new apartment becomes a part of me that I loathe to let anyone else enter. Since my divorce, as a matter of principle, I have held my *body* open to new experiences; meanwhile, my *abode* slams shut. As sexually active as I am, it has sometimes been difficult over these last three years to avoid bringing people home with me. So I've tended to get rid of sex partners quickly. It's true I can't escape from My Lover's icy grasp, but then, she exhibits no interest in my personal circumstances. Unlike Personal Ad.

"So where did you say you work, exactly?" Personal Ad asks during our third glass of Châteauneuf-du-Pape, whose blood color matches my lipstick.

"I didn't say that I work. I do have kind of a job, but

I mean, I do free-lance, you know, media stuff, here and there."

"Where, exactly?"

"Oh, around. I don't have to work just now. I'm taking this year easy, coasting a little. I'm not rich or anything, but I did inherit some money from my mother, so I can afford—"

"She's dead? When did she die, Rosie?"

"Three, four, five years ago . . . around then. Look at how your cat's crossing his little paws. That's so cute. What's his name again? I just love it when they do that."

"I haven't named him," she snaps. "Does it make you nervous to talk about your mother?"

"Me? Oh no, I can talk about anything. I'm famous—well, I was famous, well, among friends, well, if you could call them friends—for talking about everything. Especially sex, which I'm sure is far more fascinating than my mother, but whatever. Ask me anything you want, really, only first I have to use your bathroom. Excuse me." I heave myself out of the quicksand sofa.

I'm prepared. I have always been ambitious, my ambitions have been idling is all, and I have always been prepared, even when others were not. Once I *caught my mother unprepared* by visiting her without notice, the summer after college. I was considering moving to California. "What are you doing here," she said accusingly. "It's good to see you."

She dissuaded me from settling on the West Coast: "I don't think it's your style." She was busy directing a dramatization of the suffragist movement for PBS, and she didn't have much time for me. I watched her at rehearsals.

Nothing made her angrier than someone forgetting their lines. "If you aren't prepared, there's no use even going on. You're in the wrong profession, you're unqualified." But I remember her being very kind to actors who tried too hard, who threw in some unscripted hand gesture, say, or added a loud cough for emphasis. "That's not quite successful yet, but you're smart to take the risk," she'd say. Mom obviously believed in taking risks, and in being prepared.

I lock the bathroom door, extract my mini-cassette recorder from my purse. I check the auto-reverse switch, as well as the half-speed setting, to ensure that the normally ninety-minute tape will last three hours. I debate whether to put the recorder under my waistband with the tiny microphone coming up through the hole I have made on the inside of my pocket, or to wire my handbag instead and manage somehow to keep it near me. It's true that I'm wearing new lace panties, a sign that I'm prepared to be seduced and will want to remove my clothes on short notice.

I wire the handbag, and open the door before flushing the toilet. It rumbles loudly. Then I remember I actually do need to empty my bladder. I lock myself once more in the bathroom, and emerge shortly thereafter, the toilet again rumbling behind me.

"Now, where were we?" asks Personal Ad as I carefully set the handbag on the floor between us.

Before answering, I resume my sofa position, fold my hands on my lap and stretch my right thumb down to check my pulse. Fast, but not frightening. "Oh, you wanted to know about my mother. You were asking?"

"Nothing. I'm sorry, Rosie, it just seemed . . . You look different. Did you comb your hair or . . . ? To tell you the truth, you seemed frazzled a few minutes ago, and now you seem . . . calm? Or at least, calmer. Did you take a tranquilizer? Because, you know, it's your own business, but if you did, you really shouldn't drink any more wine."

I lift my glass gently by the stem. "Me? I've never taken tranquilizers, ever. Only sleeping pills. Usually if I'm very nervous, I masturbate, though of course I didn't do that either just now, ha ha. I don't know why I look different to you. Maybe you're looking at me differently?"

"Maybe." She narrows her eyes.

"Actually, I do think the world *appears* however we *see* it, don't you? The Earth used to be flat, and now it's

{42}

round," I inform her. "Cats used to be evil demons; now they're cuddly friends. Everything depends on your point of view. Well, not *your* point of view, but society's point of view. We see what we're taught to see. Yet it's true that sometimes one person, like Einstein, say, can focus a sideways glance and change the world. I'm not a relativist, I don't think just *anything* is possible. We're all bound by our personal and social histories. But those histories are always changing, that's the point. So reality is up for grabs, don't you agree?"

"I'm not sure what you mean."

A little graduate Liberal Studies goes a long way. Between French theory and the tape recorder, it's possible I will be able to leave quietly, and with dignity, after just one more glass of wine . . . No, I don't think so. I think we have passed the point of no return. Already, my gaze is slipping up her ankle, into the crease behind her knee, and over the haunted house of her thigh.

· · ·

All haunted houses remind me of my mother, as do all points of no return. Mom took me to one on my eighth birthday. A conveyer belt carried us through the dark. We stood upright, moving forward without walking, *whirrrrrrr,* as in a dream. Each of us gripped one handrail (the rails moved in tandem with the belt, as on an escalator), and held the other's hand in the middle. We passed two witches, some skeletons, one werewolf, one vampire, one Frankenstein—*Whoosh!* Cold wind blew against us, the darkness grew absolute, and the conveyer belt dipped downward as if we were falling; a voice said, "You have now reached the point of no return. *Bye-byeeee.*" I screamed and lunged at my mother. We were propelled past two heavy vinyl flaps, into full daylight. The ride was over.

Whenever we set out to seduce someone or to be seduced, it is always that point of no return to which we aspire. After that point there is no going backward, it is all going forward, no matter what, there's no more doubt. We're propelled along by an autonomous force, an irresistible force with a mind of its own, like some haunted conveyer belt, or that magic waltzing broom in *The Sorcerer's Apprentice.* Oh, okay—in reality, of course, it is we ourselves who have power over the belt, and it is we ourselves who push the broom toward desired destinations, just as it is we ourselves who must sweep up once the party's over.

Any moment now, I will rise from the sofa, take four steps toward Personal Ad, where she sits in her leather chair, put my upturned hands under her chin, and kiss her. I am no longer listening to *what* she is saying; yet I am listening to *how* she is saying it, the increasingly intimate tone of her voice. And I am watching carefully for tiny significant gestures—yes, just now, the absent-minded brush of her right forefinger across her bottom lip. *Timing* is all. Our party's not over yet.

Some years ago my graduate department hosted a party at which I reached a point of no return and succumbed to a crush on one of my professors. He and I had argued that day in class. He had been going on and on about how the 1960s had changed American culture forever, how the sixties had toppled the wall dividing politics and art, and so forth. He was one of those people who belonged to the so-called hippie generation but had never been a hippie. He repeatedly made it clear in class that *now* he took drugs, oh *now* he did—but *now,* he already had his Ph.D. and his tenure, and so *now,* it seemed to me, there were no real risks to it, no danger of losing his grip. (There are various points of no return.) The professor was trying to take personal credit for a culture he'd never participated in.

And so I raised my hand and when he paused a moment to catch his breath, I took it as a go-ahead sign, even though he had not called on me, and I said, "But isn't it an exaggeration, really, to say that the so-called *happenings* in the sixties erased the boundaries of theater, because weren't even the so-called happenings—along with so-called spontaneous theater and so-called communal theater—weren't they all just the same old traditional theater the world has always known, except on a

{45}

different stage? Because it's not as if anyone mistook these performances for real life, it's not as if anyone was really ever fooled even for a minute, so really these performances weren't radical at all —"

At which point he said, *"Would you shut up."* The classroom collapsed into silent paralysis, one student's pencil rolled off her desk but she could not move to retrieve it, we were all stricken, and then he pointed his finger at me and said, "Let me tell you something about what goes on in this classroom." He began shaking his finger. "Now, don't take this personally," he said, although it was clear that whatever he was going to say next was meant specifically, personally, for me. "Let me tell you how things work. Some of you students come into this classroom mistakenly thinking that we professors are *your fathers*" — he virtually *spat* the word *fathers* — "and you want *Daddy* to love you just for being your obnoxious self, and you want *Daddy's attention* just because you make noise — but let me tell you something, even though this will *break your heart.*"

I could hardly believe my professor was speaking in such a manner. I wondered if he might be on drugs at that very moment. Just then he stopped shaking his finger and clapped his hands once *Smack!* in front of his face, so that we were all left looking at his face instead of his finger, and then he said, "*Daddy* doesn't love you unconditionally in this classroom. *Daddy* only loves you

if you're a good student and you write a good paper."
He stopped and we all sat awestruck several seconds
before realizing it was past the hour. I swiped up my
books in a messy bundle, neglecting even to put them in
my knapsack, and ran out of the room.

My professor was a well-known scholar, an academic
celebrity (many other students had crushes on him as
well), and most certainly he had no time to attend the
graduate-department party. The professor was named
Michael. He allowed students to call him by his
first name, but nothing chummy, never Mike, or
Mick, or Micky, but only *Michael*. By coincidence, one
of my fellow graduate students also called himself
Michael.

And this second *Michael* went to the party.

I arrived late due to overpreparation: trying on different pairs of shoes; curling my eyelashes, applying mascara, curling them again; scrubbing my teeth with tooth
whitener and then breath freshener; repeatedly combing
my hair then vigorously shaking my head, and so on.
Once I finally got to the party, I immediately ascertained
that my professor was absent, and then I seized on the
second *Michael*. My husband happened to be out of
town that week, and if I had seduced the professor it
would have been my biggest betrayal ever, in fact perhaps my only real betrayal. As it was, I had nothing
to lose, never having thought much about this second

Michael. I walked up and said under my breath, "*Michael,* I'd like to see you with your pants off."

He nodded why not, later on, that night.

I found out afterward that, because he was one of the few single male graduate students in the department, several other women had tried to seduce him earlier in the school year . . . yet all had failed. No doubt their advances had prepared him for me by gradually wearing down his resistance. Often, a highway traveler will pass by three fast-food outlets before he finally gives in and, against his better judgment, takes an unnecessary, time-consuming detour to the fourth franchise, where he buys a taco he didn't want.

This Michael and I stayed until the end of the party, through some unspoken agreement, pretending to ignore each other. This made an otherwise boring party fun. It was almost as much fun as the sex we eventually had, amazingly good sex considering we were both drunk nearly to the point of oblivion. But following that night, we could never recapture the dizzying anticipation of the ignoring-each-other party, and our rapport fizzled fast.

The professor failed to pay any particular attention to me for the rest of the semester, although he wrote encouraging comments in the margins of my term paper, an essay on Andy Warhol and the popularization of art. It was my impression that by semester's end the professor had forgotten all about his Daddy speech, or at the very least, forgotten that it was I who had triggered its delivery. I didn't care. I dropped out of graduate school to pursue higher ambitions. Soon: risk and preparation.

· · ·

The tape recorder must be shutting off about now. Knowing that tomorrow I can reattend this evening's conversation—that the tape will save me from losing it all in a postdrunken blur—helps me concentrate.

"That's good. Three fingers. Curve them . . . Slower. That way, your tongue, there."

I want to, but yet—

"Keep doing that."

Told to, I must. I must, so I can. Keep doing—

Her moans get slower and longer, like the uphill chug-chugs of *The Little Engine That Could*.

"Right there—now—yes—"

Yes.

She coasts back down the other side.

For the first time in weeks, perhaps decades, I feel my anxiety lifting. Her heavy breathing softens, and I feel almost *cozy*, enveloped in warm relaxation, the kind that lingers after you've stepped out of a hot bath.

Sleepy, sleepy. Resting my head just above her crotch, feeling the aftermath pulse, may even lullaby me to sleep.

And I get so little sleep. I sink into a blissful fog, drift there, half dreaming . . . and half aware that something beneath my head shifts and lurches and then is replaced by a pillow with a cool satin cover. I feel two hands grasping me at the hipbones, and turning me onto my back. Then she puts an arm under my buttocks, lifts me up, slides another pillow under me. My internal alarm goes off.

"What are you doing?"

"You'll see."

"No. You don't have to. I liked going down on you. I don't believe in reciprocity. Really, I think you can stop."

Personal Ad stands up. I hope she's not offended. A drawer creaks open; is she getting out a bathrobe or a T-shirt? I didn't mean to make her feel ashamed or self-conscious about her body. I know how that can be. Floppy Knockers. Boom Boom Bazoom. Personal Ad is small chested, but that can create the same self-loathing, in reverse. She is crouching next to the bed. I can't see much. Now she's beside me again. She's still naked, pressing her belly against mine, touching my face with all ten fingertips.

"It takes a minute to warm up."

"What does? What are you talking about?"

"Shhh." Without leaving my skin, one hand floats

downward; fields of goose bumps bloom under her touch.

"I'm a little bit cold."

She stops, breathes inside my ear cave: "Well, *it's* probably warm by now. Raise your ass higher so I can get underneath you . . . No, higher. I want to put my head there, too. I believe in a two-pronged approach. Come on Rosie, do be cooperative."

Oh no. I hear it whirring. I *feel* it whirring, beside her tongue. Oh no, I must. I must, so I think I can, I think I can, I think I can.

• • •

The orange and black cat is curled up between us. Warm air laps my forehead each time he exhales. If I wanted to, I could slip my pillow case off and nab the animal . . . I told Personal Ad *nothing* about the paintings. And I wouldn't trust her to appreciate my disappearance, either. She might try to interfere. I don't want to hurt anyone . . . I'm so tired, my thoughts whir and skid. I just want to be famous. Someone famous once suggested writing *Don Quixote* again, but without copying it, as if one could arrive, through the maze of one's own mind, at the exact same place that Miguel de Cervantes did. As if one could *become* Miguel de Cervantes without *being* him. Genuine replication, authentic regeneration, original substitution. Surely, if one Michael can replace another, I should be able to replace myself. To become Rosie, I made a copy of a copy. Lately my mind wanders off more and more. I try to call it back, but it strays regardless, like some unhappy cat that is finally bound to run away. Oh kitty, kitty. I try to keep the cat in the bag so that no one will mistake me for crazy, or interfere.

The paintings inspire me. I know that I could perfectly recreate works like his. I plan to do something big soon; I think of role models. There's a famous young woman who does paintings of Krazy Kat as if she herself had invented Krazy Kat (like Don Quixote). There's another famous artist, a man now in his forties, who borrows and recombines disparate fragments of well-known images. Both of these famous painters are imitators of sorts, but their approaches are different: *she* would grow a tree in order to produce an apple like Eve's original; *he* would simply steal an existing apple, toss it into his fruit bowl. There I go again. Personal Ad rolls onto her side, the cat purrs.

• • •

I wake with my arms around the cat. He follows me into the dining room where I get dressed. I kiss the cat's forehead before letting myself out. In the corridor I take inventory: handbag, wallet, tape recorder, contact lens case with contact lenses, wristwatch. It's 5 A.M.

I hardly slept at all. Not because Personal Ad snored, nor because the cat began kneading my scalp; both those things comforted me. The problem was *sex*. Sometimes sex works as a sedative, and other times it's double espresso.

Sex can always go either way. At times after my husband and I made love, we would find ourselves in a huggy-wuggy mood, wherein I'd pad about in my bathrobe making oatmeal cookies, while he sat at our kitchen table reading out loud from the *Wall Street Journal*. But there were other times when sex, even very good sex—perhaps *especially* very good sex—left us on edge, leery, as if we each expected to discover at any moment that we had accidently married a dangerous criminal. Since he wasn't the argumentative type, but rather the civilized type, my husband would grow very quiet at those times and then come up with some excuse to leave the apartment for several hours.

Both elevators come to a stop where I'm waiting on the thirteenth floor, and both sets of doors slide open. It occurs to me that this only happens in older buildings, where the elevators are not yet taking computerized turns. This antiquated, inefficient system forces me to choose, like Buridan's mule, between two equal entities. The doors begin humming shut.

Whew. I had to choose between left or right. Just as now I can only go *up* or *down*. Not only can sex go one way or the other, but sometimes entire relationships run this way or that, between two poles. I press "L" for lobby, down. Before the jazz pianist, I dated a sculptor. The sculptor carved pieces of styrofoam scavenged from the street. His work was (and still is) shown regularly in the Totem Gallery. Once during the night one of his styrofoam sculptures fell off its wall hook onto the floor. Early the next morning, a cleaning woman whisked the piece into her dustpan, then into an incinerator. When he learned about it, the sculptor sent her a fifty-dollar tip. I never understood that or anything else about him, just as I never understood why our relationship skidded this way, then that way, overcorrecting each time, more out of control each time. Before it was over, we had fallen in love four times and broken up four times, within six weeks.

Even with Personal Ad, while *outwardly* our courtship appears to have progressed steadily from drinks to dinner to more drinks to sex, *inwardly* I find myself veering between attraction and repulsion. Okay, since my divorce, most of my relationships have followed this course, which can lead, on the one hand, to weepy heart-to-heart reconciliations, and on the other hand, to sudden, absolute disbandments.

Between me and my ex-husband, however, ultimately there was no warm, postcrisis reunion—*nor* any complete severance (no, not until I disappeared). For me, that's the danger of long-term relationships such as marriage: final resolutions—positive or negative—become more impossible the more impossible it becomes to believe either the best *or the worst* of the other person.

Of course the myth of marriage holds out false hope of total conciliation, and most people cling to this happy-ending idea even while they don't trust it. Sometimes the very fact of *being untrustworthy* is in itself alluring. The sculptor was a real Don Juan; I couldn't trust him at all. This enthralled me. One day he would propose marriage, the next day he would stand me up. For most of our dates, we agreed to meet first in art galleries. So at least there were various objects to ponder during the hour it always took me to realize I had been stood up.

· · ·

I feel guilty today about standing up My Lover. "You're wasting my time, Miss Fickle," she said when I called her. "I won't tolerate that."

But I need to be alone. Sex with someone new does this to me. I need to spend today as I did yesterday, debriefing myself. I took time off last night to see a show, and I've made some phone calls, jotted down a few notes, but other than that, I've been analyzing details—spying on my life. And as usual, a tape recording facilitates my work. After these two days of self-interrogation, I will tell me: A job well done, Double Agent X.

Well done, because this time, I've got the goods on Personal Ad. She thinks she's so smart with her psychology degree, and that autobiographical book she is allegedly writing. But I was like a two-way mirror; she looked right at me, spoke right to me, with absolutely no idea she was being tape recorded. Oh she tried to get the upper hand, to pry whatever she could out of me. "How do you feel right now?" she asked me point blank, when I hesitated the slightest bit before answering one of her insinuating questions. "What are you feeling right now?"

But I didn't fall for that, no, not with the tape recorder on. "Nothing unusual at all," I said. "Why, are you feeling unusual? Are you yourself all right? What are *you* feeling right now?" The hostility flying between us was unmistakable, although disguised as kindness, of course.

No wonder it takes me so long to recover myself, to restore my fragile equilibrium by reviewing, reassessing, categorizing, and recategorizing every facet of our interaction. Before I continue my work, however, there is time for a strawberry waffle with one pat of butter in the middle, where my father used to put it, and perusal of this week's *Supplément*.

Dear Readers,

Poets often commit suicide. Sexton, Plath, Berryman, Cobain, to name a few. Such deaths publicly

marry person and persona, and thus usually enhance an artistic reputation. To license this *public* marriage, however, the suicide should first, paradoxically, occur *privately*—at home with gas or gun or sleeping pills, or leaping from a secluded bridge. This lonesome aspect convinces us that the suicide is . . . *sincere*, not merely some grandiose grab for fame.

Last night, dear readers, the Chicano poet Juan Rescate killed himself in front of five hundred people; we can now expect the depreciation of his poetic career.

Rescate last year won the national Hispanic Voices Award, and was featured in *Time* magazine's Top Ten list of emerging minority writers. Yet he'd recently raised brows by telling *Time:* "We spics have too many kids and too much jewelry."

Rescate opened last night at A-Bawl with "Macho Machinations." Soon into this parody of Robert Bly, Rescate's Chicano accent began slipping away, as if he'd been training strenuously with Professor Higgins. Then Rescate fell silent, put his hand over his mouth and tore off his own mustache. With equal violence, he ripped away his guayabera and pants.

He turned out to be tightly wrapped in wide gauze, from chest to thigh. He attached one end of the gauze to a hook protruding from the podium, and pirouetted away, unwrapping himself like a top spinning free of its string.

New shapes bulged from his torso—enormous foam-rubber breasts and buttocks, held in place by a stretchy pink bodysuit. Floating on its surface was a glittering mass of tinsel pubic hair.

So who could really focus on Rescate's words when next, he said, "Excuse me, I'm going to blow my brains out."

From the tinsel, he pulled a handgun about the size of Nancy Reagan's, aimed it into one ear and fired. When the smoke cleared, a tombstone-shaped sign stood in his place:

"The Author's dead; Rescate does (not) exist. I'm no Chicano. I'm the Andorgenie."

And that, dear readers, was the end.

In the ensuing hours, efforts by me and others to substantiate any real Rescate all failed. It appears he was a fraud, someone posing as Chicano in much the same way that Asa "Forrest" Carter (former Ku Klux Klansman, George Wallace speechwriter) posed as Cherokee to write his "autobiography," a best seller.

. . .

Today's woman is fascinated by death and scandal. This week I have kept up with the news. *New York Press* carried an interview with Juan Rescate's embarrassed ex-editor at Calabaza Books: "I never actually met the man. He sounded Chicano on the phone. All evidence now indicates he wasn't authentic. We're considering withdrawing his work from print."

A *Village Voice* reviewer lamented that the poet had "cynically exploited the Latino community in a narcissistic grab for celebrity."

A guest columnist in the *Times* was also annoyed:

Only in the last few decades has the publishing industry opened its doors to writers of all races, classes, and ethnicities. The result has benefited minority communities—who can finally read their own writers—as well as the general public, always enriched by diversity. But foot-dragging skeptics will seize on any "evidence" that promoting diversity is a misguided endeavor. "Jokes" like Rescate's can have serious repercussions. For this self-promoter to blithely pursue a career in performance art—indeed, capitalizing on this controversy to further that career—is sad testimony to the increasing opportunism of today's would-be culture stars.

. . .

I'm in the large, fenced-in courtyard of a Brooklyn brownstone, surveying a crowd of political activists, and eavesdropping on two former acquaintances. They occasionally glance my way, but neither of them recognizes

Rosie. My Cultural Studies professor looks younger than I remember her. Ah, she has dyed the gray out of her hair. The civil-rights lawyer (who years ago lost a labor-union case to my then-husband) appears quite dignified, having extended his sideburns to connect with his beard.

"—typical colonial attitude. That whatever the oppressed people have, whatever it is, it automatically becomes the master's property. That's an old-fashioned form of exploitation, which is why an old-fashioned book burning will be the perfect antidote." My professor sounds just as she used to in class: cheerful and angry at the same time.

"You mean that Rescate—"

"Exactly. See, the oppressed end up having only one thing that's truly theirs."

"And it's—"

"Their oppression," she says. "Their humiliation, see, it becomes a source of pride. Sort of like 'Black is beautiful.' "

"I don't get it."

"Look. In the fifties, the PC word was 'Negro,' and 'black' was derogatory. Okay? Then Stokely Carmichael turned 'black' from an insult into an honor by declaring 'Black is beautiful.' Psychologically, he wrested a verbal weapon from the enemy and used it to fight back."

"But what's that got—"

"Minorities have to celebrate the very differences that the White Man wants them to be ashamed of. See? Minorities now realize they have something authentic the oppressor can't confiscate—it's their particular *otherness*."

"An otherness?" he says.

"Yeah, their racial or ethnic difference, whatever they're oppressed for." She impatiently shifts from one Birkenstock to the other. "Rescate stole that piece of property, see, he appropriated someone else's otherness. I mean, *she* did. Well, whatever Rescate was. *Is.* Anyway, that's the typical colonial attitude—*us* taking whatever's *theirs*."

"But why would anyone want someone else's, uh, otherness? It's not as if Rescate committed plagiary."

"Are you a journalist?"

"No, I'm an attorney with the ACLU. I'm trying to get a sense of what the . . . *crime* is here, exactly."

"A lawyer, that's probably worse."

"Someone's bringing out another basket of chicken wings. Come on. There's still time to eat before they light the bonfire. You don't have to talk to me, just get greasy with me."

"Good idea, all right, thanks."

Crossing the courtyard together, the two of them seem a good match. Both are in their fifties and wear rectangular, black-framed glasses. Both walk bent forward with heads down, as if looking for four-leaf clovers or a missing murder weapon.

After days of bickering with My Lover, and a date cancellation by Personal Ad, this public book burning promised to lift my spirits. I was cheered immediately upon my arrival by the sight of some children swinging broomsticks at a papier-mâché effigy of Juan Rescate hanged from a tree.

I pass by the piñata again on my way to the drink table. By now, its lower half has been bludgeoned off. It must be mysteriously satisfying to dismember a body, sever the limbs, saw off the head, eat the heart. As Rosie, I could get away with homicide, cannibalism, anything that appealed to me, because Rosie could disappear afterward. I once wrote an essay about two photographs by Cindy Sherman. In these works, mannequins had been ripped apart and reassembled to look (at least, to me) as though they had spent their last night with Henry Lee Lucas. I think very highly of Cindy Sherman. I reach up through the stomach, feel around the armpits, fish out a broken candy, smash it under my shoe. The satisfaction doesn't last. I head toward a banner that says "$2 MARGARITAS." Despite the giveaway price, I am the only customer.

"On the rocks, please, with salt."

The bartender's black coat appears too warm for this

mild mid-September evening, and too big for his small stature. A clump of hair nearly covers his nose, pinned there by his glasses. But he has a noble chin and (behind the glasses) brooding Kurt Cobain eyes, the eyes of someone who expects to die soon. Very attractive. He's also fast with the drink.

"Hey, you were already making this. How'd you know exactly the way I wanted it?" I stuff my dollar into a coffee can marked "DONATIONS—$2."

"It was originally for me."

I see the sign, a yard long and a foot high, taped to the table: "FIX YOUR OWN."

"I'm sorry, I didn't realize. Here."

"Your lipstick's on it. I'll make one for myself, *again,* but we're out of ice. We'll have to go to the other margarita table. What's your name?" He puts his hand on the small of my back and pushes me, as if I were a shopping cart, across the courtyard.

It excites me to be pushed around. "Sorry, I don't give out my name."

He stops. I stumble forward before stopping too.

"You don't? That's good. Why don't you?"

"For the same reason I don't answer questions. What's *your* name?"

"That's very good, I don't meet many girls like you. Drink up. It's perfect, isn't it? That's because I work as a bartender."

"So you really are a bartender?"

"Hunh. My, you're sexy."

I glance down to see what I'm wearing: purple leopard-spotted bodysuit, black vinyl miniskirt, three-inch heels. "You're sexy too, I'm sure."

He returns his palm to my back and we proceed to a table where the ice bucket's full. He glances at the tongs, then plunges his hand into the ice. I pretend not to notice.

"More."

He throws more ice into the second margarita, hands it to me.

"Aren't you going to have one?"

"Oh, sure, sure." He stares.

"You got a problem?"

"Hm? Sorry." He makes another margarita. "I was thinking—" He puts his glass down. "Why are you here?"

"I like performance art, I like scandals. I'm just here for fun."

"For fun, really? You're serious?"

"Yes, I mean no—I try to avoid being serious." He doesn't smile. "For fun, that's all," I insist, as if he had asked why I'd like to have sex with him. "I don't belong to any of the political groups here. Do you?"

"That's good. Oh, look, you've pretty well finished that one too. Take this." He hands me his drink, pats my arm reassuringly. "No, of course I don't belong to any groups either. I'm into performance art myself, in my own private, existentialist sort of way. So, I guess that, uh, nobody knows you're at this event?"

Sounds like a kidnapper's question. I lick the salt off my third margarita. "I don't know anyone here, do you?"

He holds a tequila bottle up to the lamplight—half full—and slips it into his coat. "Come on, let's book." He propels me toward a side gate.

I hesitate, struck by remorse. "We're going to miss the bonfire! I already put my copy of *Latin Longitudes* on the pile. I want to see it cremated."

"Fool," he grins as if complimenting me. "Come on." As he shoves me through the gate, I experience a numbness, not unlike that caused by chloroform, and not at all unpleasant.

. . .

My neck aches and my head feels worse. The morning light has forced its way through the oily windows into the tight, mouldy space of the back of the station wagon. My eyes sting from sleeping in contacts. My hand's asleep, squashed beneath his shoulder. I dislodge it and blow on my tingling fingers. Still numb. I slide my hand along the ceiling of the blanket suspended between us, take blind aim, lower my hand. No erection. No genitals. Gagging, I crawl forward, heave myself over the backrest into the front seat, open the door, breathe.

"Nice day, boys and girls. Isn't it?"

I turn, scowling. With his elbows propped on the steering wheel, he crams dollar bills into a baggy, raises his hip to stuff the money into a back pocket. He splutters air through his lips to imitate a fart.

"Looks like I beat you up. You've got two black eyes. I'm talking about your mascara. It's a mess. Excuse me, do you mind?"

He leans across me to toss an empty coffee can into the street. I recognize the label: "DONATIONS—$2." I get out and walk off without speaking to him.

That's a fantasy; in real life, curiosity prevails. "What's the mannequin doing in the back of your car?"

"Mom's in the textiles industry, clothing, fashion, you know. Kind of a jet-setter, my mother is. Her company uses those. I rescued that from the trash. Attractive, isn't she?"

"Looks like a male to me. And you're a good example of why I don't like men."

"You do like men. You *definitely* like men."

"Okay, but I really like women."

"Sure, fine. You'll keep seeing me."

"What, in your mom's station wagon again?"

"You seemed to enjoy it. You seemed to be swooning. At least I don't think you were just passing out.

Lucky for you I'm responsible with the rubbers. We used up two, if you forgot. Yeah, the car's okay. But I'll come over to your place for the time being."

Without glasses on, his eyes appear even more disturbed. The paintings would do him in.

"You can't."

"Aw come on, I really need a shower."

"It's your own fucking problem if you stink."

"That's good. My girlfriend never says anything like that."

"Of course not . . . Your girlfriend?"

"We've been seeing each other for three years. She lives in Boston. For that matter, so do I. But I'm breaking up with her. Not because of you, *obviously*, so don't worry."

"Okay." I wonder if he's better at blatant lying or brutal honesty. "Well then?"

"We're bored with each other, we have nothing in common. I'm more into *events* than Marcia is. Like that gathering last night. Stuff like that doesn't intrigue her. And the other thing is, Marcia doesn't think much of what she calls my *ca-reeer* choices. She's been kind of supporting me, and ahh . . . She used to work for my mom, that's how I met her. She's a career sort of girl. She's not depressed enough. I mean, she cries all the time, but . . . she doesn't like to talk about depressing subjects. She wants everything to be 'pleasant.' She doesn't like to talk about death. You know what really bugs me?"

"What?"

"She can't stand the smell of my piss. I forget to flush the toilet at night and she goes nuts when she opens the bathroom door in the morning and it smells."

"Uh-huh." I think about this. "You can pee on me sometime, if you want."

"Alright. I guess you can pee on me, too, sometime."

"But not here, and not in my mouth."

"No, of course not."

"Why *of course not?*"

He shrugs. "I just said it to placate you."

"That's not very sincere."

"I don't think you really care what I say anyway. You must be hungry. You got anything to eat at home?"

"I want to go home alone."

"Fine, get out."

"I don't even know where we are. Are we still in Brooklyn?"

"It's your bad luck you don't have a car to drive." With a businesslike air, he puts on his glasses and starts the ignition. Then he smiles apologetically.

"I give up. You can go home with me—"

"Hot shower, here I come."

"—on one condition. You have to flush the toilet every time, and close the lid afterward. And *I* don't want to discuss death either. Women are all the same. I'm going to be exactly like your girlfriend."

"Just to be mean?"

"Yes."

"Good. Sit up now so I can drive."

• • •

For the first few months after My Lover and I began dating, some two years ago, she gave me many little presents, opened doors for me, and carried my packages home from the post office. Her chivalry was impeccable, except that there was always something wrong with the gifts she chose: none of them expressed any recognition of my particular tastes. One day there was, for example, a necklace with a gold-and-garnets heart, along with a silver bracelet of colored-glass hearts. I never wore necklaces or bracelets until recently, when I became Rosie. I only wore earrings, and even so, I absolutely never wore anything with a heart motif. Not even now, as Rosie, would I do so. Heart-shaped jewelry is the quintessence of tacky, unless it's worn as a joke, like heart-shaped sunglasses. My Lover is often sarcastic but (like my mother) rarely jokes. My Lover fully expected me to wear the hearts.

Yet I'm certain that she herself would be embarrassed to wear hearts. So her gift struck me as insensitive if not, shall we say, ha ha, *heartless.* It made me feel annihilated, like some young boy who receives in the mail a frilly dress from his great-aunt who met the boy once and obviously forgot what she met.

I felt not only offended, but also unable to say so. After all, I am a polite person, and the jewelry looked expensive. I was struck dumb, incapable of protest, the way I often used to be around my mother. As My Lover blithely fastened the clasp at the back of my neck, I felt overwhelmed by indignation, helpless rage, and lust. That night I was so exhausted with emotion, I nearly fainted when she finally thought to push my legs open and lazily lower her head. I came hard within a minute after she began licking me. And then she refused to raise her head, as if I had not come at all, as if she had not even *noticed* it, and in a while I came again, harder.

While seemingly oblivious to my recent transformation as Rosie, My Lover has complimented me several times on my new assortment of high heels. Sometime soon I will do something that surprises her, that surprises everyone. Oh some people are going to be very sorry. Secret projects give me pleasure.

•   •   •

I first began masturbating in secret, around age five, using the door to my bedroom. I would straddle the open door, hold onto the doorknobs on either side, and move my pajamaed crotch up and down the door edge.

(No one showed me how to do this; I was self-taught and unpredictable, even then.) When I was about to come, I would lift myself off the floor, gripping the knobs in my hands and the wood between my thighs.

I have always needed *something other* than myself touching me, in order to climax. Nowadays, it can be a person, but for many years, humans seemed too similar to me to be *something other.* Ever since losing my virginity one drunken night in high school, I longed to achieve orgasm during intercourse, but although I tried various partners, positions, radio stations, and drugs, it didn't happen.

After my husband-to-be and I had been lovers for several months, one afternoon everything changed. I was on my back, he was thrusting energetically, my feet were resting on his shoulders, I was absent-mindedly rubbing my clit: *it happened.* And after that, whenever we fucked, *happened again.* Of course, at the moment of orgasm, I was usually fantasizing about being raped by some member of my immediate family, but that was not a problem. Not until I began *talking* about it, in therapy.

"It takes most people years to peel back the repressive layers of denial and tap into the unconscious," the therapist said. "Whereas you—well, I've never had a patient like you before. It's . . . well, it's wonderful."

Eventually, my therapist decided that, although wonderful, I had a "boundary problem." Not only did my

fantasies (the more I discussed them) open into a bottomless pit of incest, murder, and elaborate story lines
of mental and physical torture . . . but also it became
increasingly difficult to keep them to myself.

I let it slip to my husband that once in a while, when
we were making love, I would "think about something
else." He grew alarmed: "It doesn't seem private anymore. I feel like someone else is in the room with us. It
doesn't seem right. I don't think it's normal."

I told him that the more I read Freud, the more I
understood it was every woman's fantasy (conscious or
not) to kill Mommy and screw Daddy. Or vice versa.

"I feel sorry for you," my husband said.

• • •

"What time is it, Rosie?" The Bartender asks.

"Morning, obviously. You are planning to leave
sometime very soon, aren't you? I allowed you to stay
yesterday and last night because I felt sorry for you. But
as a rule, I don't like men to linger."

He has seen the paintings. If he stays any longer, who
knows what else he might find out about . . . and then I
would *really* have to get rid of him.

"My mother needs the car back Monday. Her other
one's being fixed. What day is it?"

"Sunday, but let's pretend it's Monday. You're the first
person I've let into this apartment. In general I don't

think it's a good idea. I'm not sure why I'm doing it this time."

"You're doing it to find out why you're doing it."

"Oh really," I say. "How would you know?"

"I'm surprised you didn't notice that the words I just used were yours, verbatim. Except for the pronouns, naturally. You wrote: 'I'm doing it to find out why I'm doing it.' I was reading your diary while you were in the shower, Rosie. I found it on your desk under a pile of books. You have an awful lot of art books, for someone with such bad taste. And what are you doing with seven books on serial killers?"

"You're going to be sorry. You're a real jerk, reading my journal."

"You gave me the idea when you told me you once thought maybe your husband had read your diary."

"I'm sure I said *journal*."

"Anyway, I think you were talking about your husband. You were slurring again last night. You drink too much, Rosie. You were still good in bed, though. I only read one page, the one it was open to. I didn't find out anything; it was just a fantasy. You're not a bad writer. Too obsessive, naturally, but not bad, for a girl."

"Yeah, well, *up yours*. Nothing personal, but you strike me as psychotic."

"Not as weird as you. You've got some crazy ideas about interior decoration. I've always liked weird girls.

My girlfriend's no match for this. Jesus. All this pink, and these morbid paintings, these Disney figures and clowns and shit. That's truly twisted, if you ask me."

I ignore his admiration. "I didn't ask you. You wouldn't understand. See, these paintings are my friends."

"You're not on some kind of medication, are you? Because you sound totally surreal. Speaking of which, I had a dream last night about you and my girlfriend. Want to hear it?"

"No. I want you to leave immediately."

"You're like this for a reason, aren't you?"

"Maybe."

"You want me to leave—that's fine. It's your apartment and you're the boss. That's fine. Maybe you'd like me to wash the dishes first?"

"*No.* But thanks. I like to let things stack up."

• • •

Dear Readers,

In the good old days, folks just loved Michael Jackson for being a white woman, and Madonna for being a drag queen: I say we should love the Andorgenie for having been Chicano. I suspect she predicted the public reaction over the swan song of her former persona Juan Rescate. Our reaction constitutes the Andorgenie's latest act; we are her per-

formers. We have behaved as trained. I'm not saying we're a pack of wolves . . . No, it's more like a troupe of miniature poodles. Yap yap yap!

Let's consider the chain of events since "Rescate's death." Rescate's Hispanic Voices Award was revoked, Rescate's books were withdrawn from print, and the Center for Colorful Culture held a symbolic book burning. I attended; the rhetoric was as overcooked as the Buffalo chicken. Meanwhile, the *Voice* charged that Rescate "cynically exploited" the Latino community. But tell me: What was the goal of this so-called exploitation? Poetry books don't make money. If not money, then perhaps fame? But what does it mean to be famous "as" someone else, to be anonymously famous? Moreover, Rescate, or the Andorgenie, seems to be not famous now but *infamous*.

Okay, so there was a talented person who wrote Chicano poetry without "being" Chicano. Okay, so this writer, who now calls herself the Andorgenie, once used a Chicano pseudonym. So what? George Eliot never used her proper name either, and in her own time she was ostracized for acting as a wife when she wasn't one. She played roles for which she had no legal identity—and that is why she was vilified. Haven't we gotten beyond such petty Puritanism? A hundred years later are we as unchanged as Rip Van Winkle? *Dear readers, wake up!*

Until his suicide, Juan Rescate was recognized as a talented poet, "witty, yet incisive . . . upbeat yet profound," to quote from a year-old *New York Times* review. As a journalist, I feel betrayed by the way my fickle colleagues have disowned a fine poet, merely because he wasn't himself.

.　.　.

"Most important is to be true to yourself. And it's perfectly normal for married women to have affairs," my therapist once reassured me. "What's unusual about you is that you don't keep secrets. We need to consider *why* you have informed your husband of your infidelity. Telling him about it almost seems sadistic."

That night, I told my husband what the therapist had said. "Of course you're a sadist. What you did was nothing *but* sadistic. Murder would have been less cruel. There are parts of the world where they put women to death for adultery, you know."

"They still really do that?"

"Oh yes. Absolutely," he grimaced. "They certainly do."

Yet I couldn't resist blubbering out bits of information whenever my husband would ask: "So, Sweetheart . . . how was today's session? How do you feel? Anything important or interesting come up?" I thought that if he understood me better, he might forgive me. I thought that if he could help me dig into my past to uproot the source of my promiscuity, then I could become newly pure, and my husband could love me again the way he had loved the old pure me, back when he thought I was monogamous.

My therapist asked me to tell her about my adolescence. I described the dinners I used to make according to instructions in *The Betty Crocker Children's Cookbook,* which Mom mailed to me at The House for my thirteenth birthday, after she herself moved out. There was "Swedish Meatballs," made with canned tomato soup, and "Tuna Delight," with cream of mushroom. (This all seemed normal at the time.) There were also occasions when my father cooked dinner, usually pork chops, spaghetti, or hot dogs.

Other times, he merely *planned* to cook, having invited some widow or divorcée over to The House. Those dinners always turned out the same.

Such as one steamy summer evening. By six o'clock, he'd finished off a pint of Dark Eyes. A woman with dark hair coiled high arrived, softly called my father's name through our screen door, then waited, wafting perfume and politesse. I introduced myself, and showed her past the stacks of yellowing newspapers, cartons of overdue library books, and paper bags full of trash, into an unbroken chair. I aimed the floor fans at her, and explained that Dad was napping. I went to pound on his bedroom door. I told her, "He's getting dressed." I repeated this trip to and fro, sweating more each time, until she left.

And then there were the evenings when no one was invited over to The House, we would heat up frozen pot-pies, my father would not pass out, and my brother, three years older than I, would start a fight.

We were watching TV during dinner one night when my brother lethargically leaned across the table, grasped the dial, and changed channels midprogram. After some lag time, my father responded. "We were kind of in the middle of *Bonanza,* there, son. Turn it back."

A smile twisted across my brother's face. He said, "You're drunk."

Then there was no turning back. The two of them began to swing and throw weapons from their household arsenal: saucepan, baseball bat, chair, lamp. My brother was stronger, my father more fearless. As they heaved and ducked, crashed into walls, fell down, and struggled to their feet again, my father's eyes glazed over with apathy. My brother grinned with hope and fear. I screamed vainly till murder seemed imminent, then I ran through the woods to the nearest lit house.

I came dashing back with big Mr. Coleman. My father and brother were quietly chatting. My father apologized for his hysterical daughter. Mr. Coleman withdrew fast. We finished dinner. Afterward, my brother descended to his basement bedroom like a tired vampire. My father started in on his second bottle. I watched TV with him until he confused me with someone older and wiser: "You slut. You bitch. You cheap little whore."

By next morning all was back to normal. My father burned and scraped the waffles. I took so long curling then teasing then tying back my hair that he had to drive me to school. I passed the day as a typical adolescent, cheating on exams, masturbating between classes (I brought my hairbrush into the bathroom stall), and fantasizing about death.

It was *fun* to talk about the distant past. I'd rustle up my memories and run them by the therapist like show horses in a ring, where they'd go round and round as she whipped up the questions and I kicked up the answers. Yee-haw. That evening I always related the gist of it to my husband. In the short run, this helped earn his sympathy. In the long run, it frightened him. After all, he came from a traditional Middle Eastern family. The more I talked, the more bizarre my life appeared to him, and the more certain it seemed that such a history could not fail to produce a monster, some sort of Frankenstein species, dangerous to man. My husband—ex-husband—has always been right about everything.

.   .   .

The professor I saw at the book burning used to argue that Frankenstein was "really" female, a Romantic version of Eve. Well. What is the "real" difference between male and female?

Or again, what is the difference between having sex with a man or with a woman? Besides the fact that women kiss, and generally use their tongues, better.

Just kidding. Some of my best lovers have been men. And in fact, I like to push my finger into a man's asshole even more than into a woman's asshole. Then I like to close my mouth around his cock and feel him swelling up in my mouth while I fuck his ass with my finger, or sometimes more than one finger. Sometimes my entire hand. (Even as Rosie, my nails are false, and peel off easily.) Sometimes I think I can actually feel the color inside his anus, that ripe, blood-lined pink, where the skin is so fine it is almost not skin at all. And if I'm fucking his asshole, with my other hand squeezing his balls, and my mouth sucking his cock—eventually when he comes his asshole contracts, hugging my fingers as if he truly *liked* them—and me. I like to feel liked! And I like to be hugged, even by an asshole.

• • •

Changing my look has made me unpopular. I've begun taking showers and baths at odd times in a superstitious effort to make the phone ring. Of course I disappeared to shun other people, but they might at least *try* to track me down before it's too late. I make countless excursions to PostWorld and Mail Mall, even though I receive almost no correspondence, besides occasional e-mail. I've grown so used to finding Rosie's PostWorld box empty, that this morning I whacked it shut before realizing I'd seen something inside. It turned out to be from that deluded Bartender:

> Hi there, Rosie. It rained here in Boston yesterday, it was very gloomy, and I suddenly wished it had rained the morning I woke up at your place, surrounded by all that morbid pink. I've thought a lot about the paintings, too. You're very perverted. I think you'll like the enclosed cartoon panels from a comic called *Gang Bang* by Wallace Wood. They are stupid and disturbing and there are some great pictures. He did *Gang Bang* #1 and #2 and then he killed himself. You have a very nice body. I copied down your phone number and address from the checkbook on your desk. I took your $20 because I needed it for gas.

So I've thought more about that dream you didn't want to hear. What fascinates me is a moment when you're holding Marcia down while I rape her. I've finally figured out something about Marcia.

I broke up with her yesterday. When she came by to see me I told her I no longer loved her. She responded weirdly. She brought up some money I owe her but which she knows I won't pay back. While we were talking, I felt sly. Then I realized everything was an act. We were playing our respective roles, just like in the dream. In real life, I was staring at her hand, and imagined it wrapped around my cock. I realized then that I could get her back and hurt her again. This excited me. She wanted me to. She wanted to be dominated and victimized. Unlike you, she's totally unconscious of her own desires.

I used to complain that our relationship was out of balance, that she had given me all the power. I should have recognized that's what she needed, and acted accordingly, without guilt, for her sake. She complained that she'd had similar relationships where the man was always withholding something from her. She thinks that 'something' was emotional intimacy, but it was actually more cruelty, explicit, dramatized cruelty, that she wanted. I feel sorry for her, she can't recognize her own passion.

It would be much different with you. You are less trusting and less vulnerable. Marcia opened to me right from the start, she handed me a whip though neither of us acknowledged it. We couldn't step back and see what was happening because she couldn't admit she was getting what she wanted. A basic appreciation of irony and tragedy was missing. I hope you remember telling me that we should act these things out in the theater of life. (You were drunk.) Have you noticed how 'acting out' is so maligned? People are afraid of exposing their evil natures, so they try to repress themselves and end up worse. If you're brave enough to nurture the criminal within, so am I. Even if someone gets hurt. The shaman's pain might be transfigured into grace. At least it's tied up with that.

· · ·

"So you want me to tie you down again," I mutter pensively. "Talk about predictable. Christ."

"Nothing wrong with a little conventionality now and then," My Lover says. Like most pornographers, she rarely invents new positions. She could hardly imagine the brutal twists I'm looking forward to. Oh but maybe not today. She's so childlike in her short fuzzy haircut and white cotton panties, so trusting.

"Just for your information, I *don't* feel like a spanking,

so you can tie me face up," she says. "I'd like you to decide the rest. It's your turn to take over for a while."

"Okay then. But I want you to know I'm not in the best mood just now."

"Darling, you can slap me if you want to."

"Why should I?" But I slap her anyway.

And I tie her *face down*. And I *spank* her with a rolled up magazine, saying "Bitch. Bad doggie. Bitch. Little slut. Bad girl," until I forget what I'm doing, and stop listening, even to myself. Eventually I notice we are both crying.

I stand up, decide to leave her alone. I'd rather not get carried away, yet. In her living room, I turn the television on loud to drown out her whining. I cruise until I find a *Cheers* rerun. Sam has unwittingly hired a psychopath as a bouncer. Meanwhile, Lilith is cheating on Frasier. During the station break, I investigate the refrigerator. The zucchini is too cold. (After all, I'm still a kind person, a good person, aren't I?) In the bowl on the table is a greenish banana.

I decide that after I use the banana to bring her to orgasm, I will peel the fruit in front of her and make her eat it, before untying her. This is not within the parameters of what she considers S&M; having to eat the banana may in fact disgust her. *Oh my.* Sam fires the bouncer, but Lilith fails to make up with Frasier. She decides to leave him for a "Doctor Mendel." The name reminds me of high-school biology, fluids, pressure. *Banana time.*

I didn't sleep with women until after my divorce, but then it became as habitual as any sex crime. The only unpleasurable aspect was the gloating by my so-called heterosexual so-called friends. "But what do you actually *do* with another woman?" they loved to ask. The only way to escape their prying hooks would have been to disappear, which I did.

Since then I've become more discreet. After my divorce, I fell into the habit of bar hopping and one-night stands (with both men and women; usually one at a time). But lately, while I've been *dressing* more provocatively, I've been *acting* less provocative. Maybe because I have always been contrary, or maybe because I no longer have an audience to egg me on. Or because I'm lying low, preparing to spring. The question *Why?* is never easy.

Alibis are tricky indeed, but I believe my murderous homosexual impulses can be traced back to adolescence. Like most adolescents, I loved my best friend. She was beautiful, blonde and high-cheekboned like Personal Ad, but no one noticed her because she was introverted. Shortly before we met in seventh grade, her mother had been killed by a drunk driver, which traumatized the daughter, making her shy, awkward, and unsure of herself.

I was *not* beautiful but it didn't matter. I too had lost a mother, but mine had not been slain (that would come later). So the repercussions were different. I was not shy, but *sexy.* At football games and parties, boys pursued me as naturally as dogs pursue any anxiety-ridden stranger. Back at The House, I spent nights barricaded in my room with furniture stacked against the door—but at school I wore hot pants and go-go boots.

I liked boys to ask me out. With one goodnight kiss, I felt my body levitate, like riding fast in a car over a steep bump. But what I loved *most* came later: I loved my best friend because I loved wounding her by relentlessly bragging to her about my conquests when she had none. Yes, all bragging is sadistic, just as all self-deprecation is masochistic.

•   •   •

What a pleasure this is.

I'm lapping Cool Whip off a cup of hot chocolate. I plunge my face into the cream in honor of the Three Stooges, when my phone rings after days of hostile silence.

"Rosie? Hi, it's me," says Personal Ad. "I'm sorry, I have to cancel our little outing tomorrow."

"Again?" I've got Cool Whip up my nose. "You've got to be kidding. But this was *special*." I reserved front-row seats to see the Andorgenie. "Besides, tomorrow is Halloween, my favorite holiday. Please——"

"I'm sorry. Something just came up."

"Well?"

"Well what?"

"What just came up? Did one of your clients drop dead?" Although Personal Ad claims to be writing a book, and to have a psychology degree, I enjoy reminding myself that she actually works as a mere insurance adjustor, specializing in catastrophic illnesses.

"No, it's nothing like that. What it is isn't relevant. Listen, I'm sorry. If you really want to see me, I guess you could drop by tonight."

"No I couldn't. *I'm* busy tonight." It probably sounds like a lie, but I do have plans, only can't divulge them. "Besides, tomorrow we had agreed to go *out* together, on an actual *date.* I already got us tickets for the Sin-Drome."

"Oh, I am sorry. Why don't you ask for a refund. We'll go next week."

"We *can't* go next week. It's only happening tomorrow. I know I explained that to you."

"Oh did you? I guess I forgot. My memory's not perfect. Sorry."

I lift the telephone over my head, bring it down hard against the pink bed frame. "Don't be sorry," I say out loud, then laugh at the broken receiver. Tomorrow I must try to remember to buy a new phone. *My* memory's not perfect either. Increasingly obsessed with recollections, I'm growing more and more absent-minded.

. . .

Far from being stereotypically absent-minded, several of my graduate professors exhibited perfect memory, the way some singers exhibit perfect pitch. Whereas *I* have never been able either to remember a tune *or* sing on key. Even if I hadn't dropped out of school, those professors would have remained proverbial carrots, dangling far out ahead of me.

In those pre-Rosie days my husband, too, made me feel like a donkey. His superiority constantly mortified me—yet I lived for his pats on the back. And now, without his approval to brace me, I will no doubt collapse.

In fact, the longer we're divorced, the more his virtuosity infuriates me. He knows American history better than I do, and American demographics, politics, economics, geography . . . Even his English vocabulary is greater than mine—and all this despite the fact that the United States is his second country and English his second language.

"You Americans are abstruse," I can't forget his saying

one night while we watched TV. My philosophy professor had assigned a French essay on wrestling, but I'm not good at French and so was viewing the Worldwide Wrestling Federation Championship Tournament instead.

"What does *abstruse* mean?" I humbly inquired.

"To be abstruse means to be recondite. I certainly can't make much sense out of what we're seeing."

I pointed out to my husband that the Ultimate Warrior and Macho Man Randy Savage were facing off. "So what does *recondite* mean?" I tried again.

"Oh, it's something hard to understand."

"*Don't patronize me.* Just tell me what it means." But just then the Ultimate Warrior hoisted Macho Man Randy Savage over his shoulder, and slammed him down onto the mat headfirst *Blam!* I lost my focus on verbal matters. The following morning, when the professor solicited my opinion of the French essay, I told her I had found it *abstruse*.

"That's why I am here," she congratulated herself, "to help you through the difficult passages." Back then I resented such parental figures' trying to help me through life's difficult passages. No more. Now I spend days on end soliloquizing, typing nonsense into the computer, and pretending I'm not alone.

•　•　•

I'm not alone.

"I brought him here in a taxi. He has no idea what streets we took, where you live or who you are. I told no one about this. Where do we start?" I ask.

"Here's his fee." My Lover hands me cash. "Once we get the photos under way, I promise we'll do whatever you like, Darling. Your turn."

"Alright." I palm a twenty, tuck the rest into The Bartender's pants. Behind the mask, he is not gagged but only blindfolded and under contract to remain silent— and to *forget* whatever transpires tonight.

A white backdrop hangs from the ceiling along one side of My Lover's bed, curving around its head and foot. Floodlights erase all shadows. The bed glows.

"Considering what the *Epicurean* is paying me for this work, I could afford to give *you* a nice wage too, Darling—"

"But you won't."

"But I won't," she agrees. "He—*it*—looks good." The Venetian mask is black papier-mâché with a wolfish brow, slit eyes, and a long nefarious beak. Three cameras on tripods point toward the bed, programmed to alternate shots, one photo every thirty seconds. "We have almost an hour before the film runs out. Ready?"

I lead the beast to the foot of the bed and shove him in the chest. He falls backward onto the creamy satin cover. The first camera clicks. I remove My Lover's old-fashioned barber's razor from its case. Grasping The Bartender's knit shirt at the neck, I saw into its collar, then slice the shirt down its middle.

"That's effective," My Lover notes, peering through a zoom lens. "His nipples are hard. That could mean *fear*."

Without cutting his pants, I run the blade lightly over the crotch. His jeans are so tight I could easily puncture them with the razor but don't. "It's not fear."

"New prop!" My Lover hands me a pair of elastic suspenders. I knot them around The Bartender's wrists and then throat. If he tries to pull free, he may strangle himself. Some people like that. I slip my fingers under the mask's demonic snout, touch The Bartender's dry lips. He licks my hand.

"You're wasting my time," says My Lover.

I pull off his shoes, unbuckle his belt, unzip his jeans, and yank them down, freeing his erection.

"He groaned. That's a violation."

I didn't hear any groans—just the cameras clicking every half-minute, and the continuous soft whirring of the timing device.

"Punish him."

The belt slides easily from his discarded pants. Gripping the buckle, I bring the leather down across his thighs several times. His masked head writhes back and forth. The belt is slender and supple, the kind my father used to wear. "Giddyup," I whisper.

{91}

"Quiet. Just make him comfortable."

I look at her in shock.

"Comfortable for *you,* idiot," she says.

While The Bartender remains on his back, I position his legs with the knees up, and feet flat on the bed. I climb onto one of his ankles while facing his knee. I lock my hands around the knee, press my crotch against his ankle, and rub up and down against him.

His erection bobs agreeably; a bluish vein emerges along its length. The skin of his scrotum visibly tightens. I stop, wrap the belt around his testicles and tie it. The blue vein darkens.

"Ready and at your service."

"Alright. Now put this on—by itself."

I stand on the bed, straddling The Bartender, and strip for the cameras. Then I tie the apron behind my waist. It's short and white, with a flounced ruffled hem. *"Vous désirez quelque chose?"* I curtsy.

"Très adorable," she says, "but we're just making photos, no soundtrack." My Lover remains dressed in black pants, tuxedo jacket, and wing-tip shoes. "Please be seated."

I sit on The Bartender's groin, upright and facing him. His penis now protrudes from between my legs: *interesting.* I arrange my apron to enhance the illusion that the penis is mine. My Lover steps onto the bed and sits down astride The Bartender's chest, facing me. For a moment we're riding a raft hell-bent for a fall. Instinctively I reach for The Bartender's cock.

"A present." My Lover dangles before me what looks like a child's smooth plastic bracelet.

"Oh, of course." It slides right over the flanged head, down to the base of the shaft. Then I close my fist around the bracelet and pull.

"Stop it," My Lover says, leaning toward me. While she and I kiss, I keep my right hand on The Bartender's erection, glide my fingers over its taut skin, feel its pulse. My left hand strokes the inside of My Lover's thigh, then ventures under her jacket.

"Goose bumps. Is that fear?"

"More props!"

I let go of The Bartender to unbutton My Lover's jacket: no shirt. In her inside jacket pocket, I find a pair of pincers. I hold them up for the cameras: they're gold, connected by a chain. I clamp them onto her nipples.

"Aren't they beautiful?" she shudders.

I unbutton her pants: no underwear. I bend toward her—pinning The Bartender's hard-on beneath me— then change my mind. I gesture for her to trade places with me. She hesitates.

"Anything for your pleasure."

She and I sit facing each other again; the penis now appears to be hers. I flex my ass muscles against The

Bartender's pectorals. The mask snout presses into my back, between my dimples. I lean over, take My Lover's cock in my mouth as far as possible, get it very wet.

I come up for air, crawl forward, maneuver my feet alongside My Lover's hips and lower myself onto the gleaming erection. I press my mouth against My Lover's ear to amplify my moans as I lift myself up and down, higher then lower, until the current traversing the three of us grows so strong I no longer know where we're going, who's with whom, or which one's me.

I think I hear someone saying *Stop,* but I don't.

. . .

I had decided on velour hip-huggers for Rosie's first official *date.* But since Personal Ad stood me up, it's pointless to play debutante. So I'm wearing the same crusty sweatshirt and shapeless leggings I lounged around in all day, mulling over last night's rendezvous, reading true-crime books and looking at the paintings.

This is the first time that I have returned to the SinDrome since attending Pet Night with My Lover two years ago. I remember she dressed me in old Playboy bunny ears, a fake-fur swimsuit and wooly boots. I found it tacky, but My Lover and I never agree on aesthetics.

Before I left her Soho loft early this morning, we argued about the Andorgenie: "That sort of sexual the-ater was exhausted in the seventies, Darling, and it wasn't new then either. The Futurists proved long ago that anything could be packaged as *art*. Your taste is hopelessly backwards. Nowadays one must turn *art* into *real life*, not the other way around."

So there's no danger of running into My Lover at the SinDrome tonight. I can devote full attention to the mystery at hand. The theater grows dark.

A spotlight shows a man wearing an Elmer Fudd mask, standing behind a podium. "Yes, it's me. Ready to be read to? The Bible, if taken metaphorically, freed from the chains of the literal, contains all the wisdom we need to live by . . ."

The Andorgenie reads soothingly. " '. . . Now I rejoice in my sufferings for your sake, and in my flesh I complete what is lacking in Christ's afflictions for the sake of his body, that is, the church . . .' "

The biblical words must be profound. The idea of profundity plunges me into a stupor, groggy with solipsistic daydreams, unable to listen.

Floor lights come on from underneath the podium, revealing the Andorgenie's lower half *through* the podium, which turns out to be transparent, glass or plexiglass. Oh not again. It's one of *those* things: he's masturbating while he reads.

Floodlights sweep the stage. To the Andorgenie's left, a settee—no, it's an actual pew—on which two nude black women are lying intertwined, kissing. One wears short, bleached-orange hair. The other has dreadlocks. Silver rings dangle from her pierced nipples. These women are the sort of tough and gorgeous dykes I used to admire at the Clit Club, before I stopped going, before I became Rosie. I feel my muscles tightening, and cross my legs.

The Andorgenie stops reading. Holding his erect penis, protruding through his open zipper, he approaches the women. I feel as though I've seen this before. One of them leans forward, saying "Aww," reaching out to pat its puppyish nose.

She rips it off and throws it to the audience.

"Rye bread! Take some and pass it on!" she shouts. When the loaf reaches me, I break off an extra piece, to save for Personal Ad. Then I remember her attitude. I wad the bread into a little pellet and toss it blindly up and behind me. I hear someone a few rows back let out a small scream.

The castrated Andorgenie is now rolling on the stage floor, squealing and clutching his crotch. I would be glad to call it a night. But suddenly, a new figure flies in from offstage, suspended in midair: a human-sized Tinkerbell, astride an overturned Eiffel tower.

Magnified static, then mangled music, as she lip-synchs: *"I'll be there . . . I'll be there . . . I'll be there . . ."* It's the literal, not metaphorical, sound of a broken record. The stage curtains close, the record stops, the house lights come on.

I struggle to my feet, disoriented. People around me break into conversation. I rise on tiptoe to scan the crowd for anyone I know, then remember I'm Rosie; no one knows me. I leave seething over the Andorgenie conundrum and involuntarily humming that song, "Just call my name and I'll be there . . ."

Outside, the anonymity of the city consoles me. Walking home on Bleecker Street, I begin to feel inexplicably buoyant, as if I had just won an election or a new car — as if Personal Ad had not stood me up. Everything looks different. Passersby appear to me as so many magical creatures, kings and queens, ghouls and witches. "The evening has turned out to be a religious experience," I exclaim.

Well it is Halloween.

$$\bullet \quad \bullet \quad \bullet$$

"At some point, your demons will resurface. You're disguising your inner turmoil in a show of false confidence," my therapist warned me some three years ago. "It's not wise to quit in the middle like this." She was right. (They always are.)

It was the day I divorced her, the day after my husband divorced me, leaving me bereft of his health insurance, among other things. My therapist declined to offer me a discount. "It could adversely affect your treatment. So it's in your best interest that I don't. And it's in your best interest to continue therapy. There's a lot of material we haven't covered yet."

"How would you know about it?" I said. "How would you know about anything we haven't already talked about?"

"I'm referring to life periods—"

"Menstruation?"

"Your sense of humor continues to be a vehicle for hostility." Oh yes, she was right. "But very well. For example, starting before menstruation—your prepubescence. That's just one epoch that we have yet to delve into with sufficient thoroughness."

I cannot remember much prior to sixth grade. They say it is difficult to recall a painful childhood, but for me, being contrary, it's the happy times before my mother left which I have trouble remembering. Okay, maybe I wasn't happy, maybe I was only pretending. But what was I really, then? I was smart, okay.

At the age of nine, I solved a riddle my paternal grandfather posed at the Christmas dinner table. He was a famous, Pulitzer-prize-winning Broadway dramatist. My grandfather's renown explains why my mother married my father. But the family name was not lost on me, either, not even in prepubescence; already, I knew that notoriety meant everything.

It was generally assumed my father would someday be famous as well. Both he and my mother acted for years as if he were *already* famous, hobnobbing with well-known playwrights, actors, and critics, riding on my grandfather's coattails. Over the years, their illustrious so-called friends fell away, as it grew obvious my father would never be more than a drama professor—never his father's proud successor but merely the inferior son—and so finally my mother jumped ship.

Without her to keep him afloat, my father swiftly sank into the vodka depths whence he has never returned. My mother's second husband died without earning much acclaim either. But my mother did go on to make a respectable name for herself, directing historical movies for TV. She probably realized that my father's meager efforts to break into Broadway had been doubly useless—since in any case, no one takes Broadway seriously anymore.

But there was a time when Broadway glittered with possibility, a time when my family basked in heartwarming optimism. For many years, my grandfather's name appeared regularly in the *New Yorker, Vanity Fair, Life* magazine. Back then, the aura of my grandfather's success enveloped us all. As a prepubescent child, I could be hundreds of miles away in Ohio and still sense it. Pouring milk on our cereal, my brother or I might say, "Granddaddy takes *cream* on his oatmeal." *Shazam!* We'd perceive golden light enveloping us as clearly as Cellini saw his own halo. We didn't snatch at the miracle with any outbursts of "Isn't cream expensive?" or "I want cream on *my* cereal." No, because back then, the mention of our grandfather was enough to bring even my brother under momentary control.

So I was demure when, at Christmas dinner, after I had whispered the answer in his ear, my eminent grandfather announced, "She's a little Einstein. I've known grown men to spend hours on that puzzle. She figured it out right away."

Lately I've been trying to figure out Personal Ad. Many times I have played the tape recording of our night together, listening for clues. I don't want to hurt anyone; I just want to be famous, and in control. I didn't like the way she stubbornly circled certain subjects. I listen again and again to the bullying, intuitive nature of that circling, like the circling of her tongue later on, its pitiless search. Hmmm. Also, there is something not on the tape, but which I remember clearly. I was running my index finger down her spine, when she repeated back to me a sentence I'd said hours earlier: "It gives me the hot chills when you do that."

"You sound exactly like me. You're imitating me."

"That's a paranoid attitude," she replied in a tone that made me think I was right. In fact, it seems to me that I have noticed Personal Ad mimicking me at various times, both in bed and out. I suspect that impersonation is her secret hobby, her way of maintaining the upper hand.

I remember the riddle like this:

You are on your way to a town called Reality. You are almost there, but then you come to a fork in the road, and don't know which way to turn. You know that one direction must lead to Reality, and the other to a town called Illusion. But you don't know which way leads to which town.

A man is standing at the fork in the road. You know that he must be from one of the two towns, but you don't know which. You also know that *all* the citizens of Reality tell the truth *all* the time, whereas the residents of Illusion *invariably lie* whenever they speak.

You are allowed to ask the man one question. If he is from Reality, he will answer honestly; if from Illusion, he'll lie. But since you don't know which town he is from, you won't know whether he's lying or telling the truth. It has to be just one question, whose answer—whether the truth or a lie (and you'll never know which)—would tell you the right way to go.

The answer is, *Which of these two roads takes you home?*

Whichever road he indicates, is the one that leads to Reality.

You see, if he's a liar, he has to lie, so he cannot point toward Illusion, his real home; he will have to point in the other direction, toward Reality. If, on the other hand, he's a truth-teller, well then he lives in Reality, and will point toward Reality also.

The way I have been feeling lately, any situation could become a turning point. I don't want to end up in Illusion, like my brother . . . but the paintings have begun to appear alarmingly real. And they were done by a famous man. Well, I won't put that kitty on the table unless it's a sure bet, as they say. And, as they say, the game's always changing.

.   .   .

"I brought champagne."

"How inspired. What put that idea into your little head?"

"Celebration time."

"How delightful. Of what?" asks Personal Ad.

"Us getting together. I left the phone disconnected all day so that if you tried to call and cancel again, you couldn't reach me."

"Isn't that thoughtful. Do come in."

"Thank you, thank you," I bob my head. "I'm so polite."

Personal Ad falls coldly silent. She accepts my leather coat, drapes it over a chair, sets the Veuve Cliquot on the rug, and lights a cigarette. I automatically take my usual place on the sofa. She begins pacing back and forth. Her cat leaps off a bookcase onto the cushion beside me. I stroke his chin. The cat's face is orange, with a triangular black patch over one eye. "So, little pirate," I coo absent-mindedly. "Been murdering and plundering, have you? Was there blood everywhere?" The cat stretches out on his back. I pat his tummy, while thinking of ways to injure Personal Ad.

Personal Ad is wearing a heavy skirt that swishes loudly while she paces. I would like to engage in conversation, because I have prepared a fine topic: the influence of rock music on modern orchestration. It took an hour of research. When she points out that Stravinsky is the century's most important composer (which she has mentioned before, as if casually), I will throw back that it was not Stravinsky, but Led Zeppelin. That's the sort of insane yet plausible idea that's impossible to argue with. So much for her psychology degree.

Unfortunately, it seems that the conversation, so well rehearsed, may never take place. Personal Ad continues pacing, her skirt swishing, as if she had forgotten me.

"Look, I know you have a lot to think about, but

why don't you think about it some other time? Everyone's got problems. You're not the only one with problems. Maybe you shouldn't invite people over if you're just going to swish and swoosh back and forth like that. Just because you're writing some book about your own problems doesn't give you some special license to act superior—woo, woo, woo, the big psychology-degree genius too busy to talk to her own guests."

Personal Ad stops, wheels toward me, grips my hand and pulls me several yards, into her bedroom.

"Lie down."

I don't understand her. I lie down. As if on cue, I feel tired.

"Don't go to sleep."

I would like some champagne, but I say nothing. I would also like to unbutton my jeans, which are too tight. I try to avoid petty thoughts like the fact that my green rayon blouse is wrinkling under my back.

"Listen." She stands over me, puffing on her cigarette. "I'm fully convinced by now. You need help."

Maybe it's not too late to turn this around: "Help me if you can, I'm feelin' dow-ow-own. Help me get my feet back on the grou-ou-ound. Won't you pleeease, pleeease help me, help m—"

"You're awfully out of tune. Now pay attention: you need therapy."

{104}

That's it, I can forget the champagne. "Look, I've tried therapy, it doesn't work. Hey, since that Beatles song just happened to come to me right now, let's talk about rock music and its hybrids. What do you really think of Frank Zappa? Or for that matter, Leonard Bernstein? Or Pierre Boulez?"

"I see." She sits down in a chair beside the bed, glares at me with her brilliant blue eyes, kicks off her shoes, smooths her skirt, squashes her cigarette in an ashtray. "I'm convinced you need help." Personal Ad picks up a book from her night table, as if preparing for a bedtime story. "We'll start now. Please close your eyes until I tell you to open them. Are you comfortable?"

I have lost. I surrender. I shut my eyes. My mind empties, and as if to accompany the lost contents, my body heat rushes out. "I'm a little bit cold." I feel a blanket settling over me. "Thank you."

"You're entitled to that."

I wait but she says nothing else. I hear the book pages turning. A minute passes. "Well?"

"Well what? I'm waiting."

"Oh . . . I don't know what to say."

"Maybe you would like to explain why you're afraid of therapy."

"I'm not *afraid* of anything," I inform her. "That's not the point." Like most psychology scholars, Personal Ad understands nothing about the human psyche. "See, to me, therapy's like pantyhose."

"Mm-hmmm?"

"Okay, listen. They could make pantyhose to last forever but they don't. Pantyhose are *designed* to tear and run all too easily, so that you have to keep buying more. And you have to keep buying more because even on hot days, you begin to feel naked without pantyhose. Therapy's the same way. See, therapists keep coming up with new kinds of addiction—food addiction, work addiction, sex addiction. They even invented what they call codependency, which is being addicted to other people. *Which* other people? Basically anybody and everybody except your therapist. The only things you're allowed to be addicted to are therapy, therapeutic drugs, and therapists. But nobody's talking about this *therapy addiction,* which is actually an expensive and debilitating habit, much more costly than pantyhose."

"I see. So you wear pantyhose?"

"Hardly ever any more, not the plain ones. I mean, I wear fishnets, lace tights, stuff like that, but not, you know, regular hose."

"Hmmm. It's interesting then, that you would be thinking about something that you hardly ever use."

I hear more book pages turning, and then what sounds like her finger tapping the paper. "Here we are: *This may be a case of regression, or repression, or reaction formation, or projection, or introjection, or reversal.* It's certainly some form of denial . . . *But the defense mechanism is always its own undoing.* Well. No doubt you're unconsciously thinking of something, or someone, from your past."

"Not that I know of. Say, we could open the champagne."

"I remind you of your . . . mother, perhaps? Did your mother wear pantyhose?"

"Of course."

"Of course?"

"Her generation, they just did. They didn't have any choice. Look, at least put it in the refrigerator, for later."

"No choice." I hear the crackle of paper again, then Personal Ad clucks her tongue as if in pity. "Ah yes. *The rhetoric of the obsessive compulsive invariably imagines a lack of choice. This may at times be related to a form of melancholia, in which the absent figure* (your mother, probably) *is internalized, so to speak, and gives orders from within.* Ah yes. No choice. So . . . If your mother had tied you up with her pantyhose, would you have had any choice?"

"Uh, um, what?"

"Let's see now." More crackling. "Mm-hmmm. *Whenever the ego is threatened, the patient may unconsciously gesticulate in order to convey an otherwise suppressed response to the therapist's questions.* Well now Rosie, I see your mouth is twitching. Are you nervous?"

"No. As a matter of fact, I'm thirsty. But just the idea—"

"You're not nervous? You're not uncomfortable?"

"No, thank you. The blanket's perfect. But I would like—"

"Good, or as you say, *perfect*. So then we'll do a little test."

I hear the book slam shut, and then a drawer opening and closing. I remember the sound of that drawer; Personal Ad must be getting out that electric massager which heats up. What she called her two-pronged approach. Oh yes, oh definitely yes.

"Now, let's see if this sound means anything to you, Rosie . . . Do you recognize it?"

"There's nothing yet. Are you sure it's plugged in? I can't hear anything."

"Try harder. Now?"

"No, yes. You aren't . . . What are you doing?"

"What do you think? What does it sound to you as though I'm doing?"

"You aren't . . . aren't . . . It sounds like you're gathering up the leg of a pair of . . . pantyhose, the way you would . . . put your thumbs in and then bunch up the sides of the hose, you know, as if you were going to put them on, that scratchy sound."

{108}

"Excellent response. Also happens to be correct. Just a minute more. Just a minute . . . Let me just . . . There. Open your eyes."

Uh oh. She has put the pantyhose on, one leg over her head, the other leg enmeshing her right arm. She presses her tongue against the transparent net and I feel faint. She raises her arm and spreads her hand, so that the webbing stretches between her fingers as if she were a giant reptile. I'm compelled to undo my own buttons.

• • •

Compulsions often undo me. For the moment, however, I am perfectly restrained.

"I'm doing this to find out why I am doing it." I have been talking to myself a lot lately. Not only talking, but *lying*. My motives are invariably darker than I can admit.

I go back and forth in the rocking chair in my bedroom. My bottle of nail polish matches the rose-pink rocker. I stop to insert cotton balls between my toes, thinking of the movie scene where Humbert Humbert paints Lolita's toenails. I've rarely sampled older men, besides my ex-husband. The Bartender is two years younger than I am.

My toenails are almost dry when the intercom sounds. I trot gingerly to the control panel, buzz him into the building. I lean over the hallway bannister to watch his head zigzag up the stairwell. There's his black coat.

"Nice to have you here again, I'm sure, but no stealing. Maybe you noticed I subtracted twenty dollars from your thespian fee the other night. Which we won't discuss."

"God, I thought I'd never get here."

He crushes my head against the wool coat. I push him off. He follows me inside my apartment, shuts the door behind us and drops his coat on the floor.

"So you're here. Drive your mother's car?"

"What is it with you and my mother's car? I took the train. You look great, Rosie. But you should get rid of this artwork. I have some more ideas about how to do it."

"Don't rush me. It takes time to get inside the head of someone disturbed."

"Jesus, you're really into that stuff. Come here."

"Maybe in a minute." I reach down to retrieve the cotton from my toes.

"I brought you that book you wanted on Duchamp. We can talk about it later, if you want. Your feet look sweet like that, really adorable."

"Thank you. I got it from a movie. Did you know that Humbert Humbert loved Lolita so much—"

"Look, would you come here?"

"In a minute." I head for the refrigerator, open it. "Let's see some of your bartending skills."

He comes up behind me and slams it shut. I turn to say, "Temper, temper," or even, "Fuck you."

Instead, I say, "That's right. *You* come *here*."

• • •

Hi there, Rosie. I'm on the train home now. It's dark out. Aren't you scared how we'll end up? Saturday's such a blur. Maybe you've forgotten how we started fucking on the cold kitchen floor and it was so intense that you had to stop to smoke some weed. Then we exhausted ourselves and tried to take a nap but couldn't, like in nursery school. I'd been frantically building fantasies of you all week, and I came that morning really quickly. You were so turned on I assumed you had already had 10 orgasms. I hope you haven't blacked out anything. After you got drunk at that bar where you guessed three people's names right, you made me go buy enemas—for the 'poor little ones' since your drugstore was out of the adult kind, before we came home and put on the first video. I liked fucking you with dildos and watching porn (by the way, I've got your *Café Flesh,* just borrowing), but the best was the à la carte fuck, when I looked into your eyes no frills fuck. Don't you believe in ANY authenticity?

Was it that night or the next day that we gave

each other the enemas. It slipped so easily into your little asshole. (Uh oh, an old Chinese woman just sat next to me, I hope she doesn't read English.) Where was I? We talked about the paintings and serial killers. You made me cook for you, steak Saturday, lamb chops Sunday, and the fried egg, toast, bacon, juice (so particular!) whatever morning it was you went out for the paper, to check our horoscopes. 'Be wary of blind passions,' mine said. So you blindfolded me ~~just like the night we went~~ You fucked me with your strap-on, and then you fucked me as if you were a woman. God, your period! Afterward you wrapped a warm, wet paper towel around my cock—I can't stop imagining myself like this, stretched out, hand-cuffed with an erect, bandaged, bloody cock. The image lures me toward death, like when you ordered me to hate you while fucking. It led to a thrilling rage I can't remember having access to. I thought of Nazis and Jews. Who was which I don't know. I almost spit in your face just before I came. Then you took my head in your hands so that my head wouldn't break apart. I needed you to bring me back. I slept like I was drugged and when I woke you said something about your father but as usual were cryptic and secretive. At some point we were fucking and you slapped me. I liked it but don't like it that when I look at you the side of my face asks to be slapped again. Why do you insist we confront hate but see love only as a last resort?

· · ·

Out of love for his fickle stepdaughter,
Humbert Humbert resorted to slaughter.

Sometimes there's just no rhyme or reason. My Lover is not the jealous type . . . but yesterday she accused me of making eyes at a handsome young waiter. If anything, I thought *he* was making eyes at *me*. My Lover and I had finished dinner and were pondering what to order for dessert. Her left hand began inching up my leg while her right hand held the menu. I glanced up and found the waiter staring. I stared back. He did not flinch, but My Lover did.

"You're flirting with our waiter. You're not really a lesbian, are you?" she said—which was odd because I have never claimed to be one.

Later that night, while My Lover slept and I lay awake with insomnia, I thought everything over. I had been falsely accused, for I had not been flirting. While returning the waiter's stare, I had blinked, which My Lover probably mistook for a *wink* because my Maybelline Extra-Thick Marathon Mascara eyelashes momentarily stuck together. Surely that explained everything. But my own innocence did not comfort me—quite to the contrary, it had the unsettling effect of putting My Lover in the wrong. That would not do.

So today I have donned the same spandex miniskirt to return to the restaurant. I arrive early, about 5 P.M., and am the only customer. I sit in the chair I sat in last night.

"Good evening," he says. He looks Mediterranean, with narrow hips, olive skin, and curly black hair like my ex-husband's.

"Hi. No thanks, I don't need a menu."

"Ah. You know what you would like to order?"

"Nothing."

". . . Can I get you something to drink while you're considering what you'd like to eat?"

"I don't want any food, thank you."

"Shall I bring you the wine list?"

"No, but thank you very much."

"You're very welcome. So . . . what is it that I can bring you?"

"Would you mind sitting down, right here, for just a second?" I motion to where My Lover was seated some hours ago. He sighs with self-pity, pulls the chair out, and perches on the edge. I smile to convey warmth and friendliness.

"Would you like to put your hand up my skirt?"

He jumps to his feet, knocking over the chair. "I'm sorry, I—No, it's you who should be sorry. You must leave immediately. I know what you are. I saw you in here last night."

"You know what I am?"

"Get out, now, I'm serious, or you will be — Now leave!"

I have never stayed where I'm not wanted. On the way out, I pick up a ceramic dish containing toothpicks. Some yards away, I turn and throw it at the restaurant's oak door. It bounces off the wood and falls into the soil surrounding a potted evergreen. The toothpicks scatter. Temper, temper.

·　　·　　·

Repetition seems inescapable. Night after night I have paced to and fro, exhausted, wide awake, staring at the paintings, thinking *it's got to stop*. The last straw stands in for all the other straws. I chant, "A stand-in! A straw man!" I need to devise some foolproof way out.

"If I only had a brain!" I can't even carry a tune.

While washing my face this morning, I glance into the mirror and see that the light-brown roots of my hair are exposed almost a full inch. Why didn't I notice this earlier? I don't want to blow my cover.

I apply a squeeze bottle of dye to my hair, pull a plastic cap over my scalp, put in my contact lenses to better read *Le Supplément,* and settle into a hot bath to wait for the dye to set. Oops. I wring out *Le Supplément,* hang it to dry. With a pumice stone, I sand down the callouses on my feet. I think of the bloody severed feet in Georg Baselitz's paintings. Some men stop at nothing.

I think of other extremities.

I step out of the bath to retrieve the nail clippers, razor, under-eye cream, skin-firming tonic, and tweezers. I am plucking the half-dozen dark hairs that sprout around my nipples when the phone shrieks. It no longer rings properly due to the crack in its spine. I couldn't remember to buy a replacement, so I wrapped the receiver in masking tape. It looks like one of those ancient cat mummies you see in museums. I hurry to answer it, in case it is Personal Ad returning my numerous messages asking her out.

"Rosie, why haven't you called me? You haven't talked to me for weeks. What about our plans? Didn't you get my letter?" It's The Bartender.

"Yeah. So what?"

"Well did you like it?"

"It wasn't exactly inventive. You didn't make anything up. Not that you got everything right, either. Yeah, maybe I liked it."

"Of course you did. You're nuts about me. I'm coming down to see you again the weekend after next."

"Wait a minute. Says who?"

"Come on, you want me to. I know you do. It's been three . . . no, four weeks already."

"You're wrong. Only three."

"Jesus, considering the last time we spent together, the stuff we did—"

"That's not my problem," I remind him. "Anyway, if you're so eager, what's wrong with this weekend? We can go see the Andorgenie. I have to get to the bottom of this before I make some big mistake. If you really want to get serious, I think you should help me. We can snoop around together backstage."

"Love to, but I can't. I'm busy. I'm coming down the weekend after next, like I said."

"Whether I want you to or not?"

"If you put it that way."

"You probably rape schoolgirls, too."

"That's your fantasy, not mine." He sighs forlornly, reminding me of his haunted eyes. "Not that there's anything wrong with schoolgirls," he adds more cheerfully. "I'll be there sometime Saturday. If you're not there, I'm going to let myself in and wait."

"You don't have a key."

"I don't need one. I work as a locksmith."

"I thought you worked as a bartender."

"Oh, right. But I make a little money on the side doing, you know, locksmith jobs. I do a lot with my hands. I thought you noticed."

Shortly after I hang up the phone, it shrieks again. Again, I pounce. Again, it is not Personal Ad.

This time it is my brother, calling from The House. Even though he and my father are among the few people who have Rosie's phone number, I am surprised to hear from them this morning. For many years, I have sent birthday cards, Christmas presents, and monthly phone calls their way, without anticipating anything in return. Probably I am motivated less by good will than idle curiosity, like those NASA scientists who send friendly messages into outer space despite the unlikeliness of any aliens responding. No, that's wishful thinking on my part, pretending my father and brother are of a different species than me.

And anyway here's my brother's voice, coming in via AT&T: "How's that city life? Any worms in the Big Apple?"

My father and brother know nothing about my being Rosie. Not that it would make much difference to them. Nearly two decades, and they haven't seen me at all. Yet lately I find myself going back, reliving what followed my mother's departure.

Of course, my family had resided in the same two-story house, on a five-acre plot of Ohio woods, for many years. But it was only after my mother ran off with the chairman of my father's drama department that a *force field* sprang up, creating The House. It was precisely *then* that gravity increased; the floor became hypermagnetized. From then on, objects fell and stuck to it—towels, books, dishes, newspapers, bottles, cans, unopened mail, spoiled food . . . Most of our furniture also snapped, toppled, or sagged floorward. For some weeks now, every day at 3:30 P.M. I lie face down on the kitchen floor, overwhelmed by the memory of my body growing heavier the moment I entered The House each day after school. Usually it was all I could do to drag myself to my room, lock the door, and bulldoze through the piles of clothes, magazines, and hair curlers to the bed, where I would lie still as a giant slug until evening.

Nowadays I'm an incurable housekeeper, straightening my underwear drawer, dusting the paintings. But back then, the only tidy place in The House was my brother's room. Within the first month after my mother's flight, he covered his walls with dozens of maps, all neatly Scotch taped or push-pinned in place, and dozens of clocks, all set to the same, correct time.

On all the maps, my brother marked the location of The House. Like me, he has always been ambitious: the maps varied in range from our township, to the United States, to the entire solar system. Sometimes my brother drew in The House as a rectangle, with an isosceles triangle on top. Other times it was a red paper dot stuck on the planet Earth.

On his desk, a chess game was perpetually in progress; my brother played both sides. He kept his room bathed in white light twenty-four hours a day, using ten or so lamps with bare light bulbs. An insomniac like me, he slept with wax plugs in his ears and black patches over his eyes, pirate style.

After I left for college never to return, my father passed out at work for the fourth time and was fired. My brother was repeatedly arrested for burglary, until finally they put him in an asylum for a couple of years. He never stole anything. He merely broke into a few buildings in order to destroy fluorescent lamps, believing they were an offense to God. While institutionalized, my brother promoted himself to the position of God. He left the asylum *as God,* but nevertheless resumed living in The House.

It has been more than twenty years since my parents' divorce. My mother's second husband died in late middle age of a heart attack, and my mother spent the remainder of her life in California, unattached.

My father refers to himself as a *retired widower.*

But me, I try to live in the here and now, taking the present as a given. So now I try to listen to my brother, who picks up where we left off last time, patiently laying out for me the mathematical evidence that he is God. "It's like Fermat's last theorem. I've known for a long time that I was God, and now finally I can prove it."

My brother's proof involves historical dates, numbers in the Bible, his birthday, and so forth. Like many women, I'm afraid of math. It all adds up. I tell him, "Mm-hmmm" and "It sounds possible." He appreciates that. As we bid our goodbyes, he says, "I love you," as he always does. Usually I respond with "Take care," or "Best wishes to you and Dad," or "Be good to yourself," but this time, for the first time, I answer, *"I love you too."*

And as I say the words, I finally remember where and when it was that my brother told me "I love you" in the same voice he used just now. It was that summer day long ago when he had decided that we should try sexual intercourse. Brandishing a coil of rope, he had said, "I love you. I love you. I love you . . ." with that same intonation.

While I ponder this discovery, the telephone hundreds of miles away in The House is transferred from my brother to my father. For no reason, thoughts of Personal Ad flit along the horizon of my consciousness.

"Are you there?" my father asks.

We talk about the news. We can do that because my father is coherent until around noon, his third drink. We

{121}

discuss a group of soldiers in some other country whose excuse for breaking a civilian's arms and legs was that he had thrown a rock. We agree this excuse is lame. Then my father says: "It makes no sense. It's like an axe murderer telling the judge, *Okay, I killed and dismembered her, but I never took her bra or panties off or looked at her vagina or breasts.*"

"Yeah Dad, it makes no sense."

At least no more sense than it ever has, my father's peculiar way of saying things. I owe much to my father, including my love of the absurd, which gives me pleasure. I am an art *hobbyist,* a murder *buff.* My father never tells me he loves me, of course, but without thinking, this morning I incongruously declare, *"I love you too,"* after which I unplug the phone.

Ho hum. Or, as my father likes to say, "Hi ho."

I throw on my bathrobe and raise the shades; you close one door, you open another.

The weather's dark. The interiors of several well-lit apartments are easily visible. In the spirit of anonymity, I have avoided letting my neighbors see me. But hell. "Hell," I say again, this time out loud. I switch on the lamp beside me, place my desk chair before the window, and sit down.

Across the street and to the left, a young woman eats a sandwich while standing at her kitchen counter. In the apartment below hers and to the right, an elderly Oriental couple sit at a table spooning soup. It is already lunch time, and I am not yet dressed.

Ah, I am not alone. One floor above the couple, directly across from me, I spy a man in his Jockey briefs, cleaning his living room. I watch him bend over to get something from under a coffee table. I laugh contemptuously, I don't know why. I watch him straighten up and frown. He lifts the coffee table, moves it several feet, cleans the floor there, shoves the table back. He wipes his forehead with his wrist. His hairline is receding. He glances up—and registers my presence. I resist the urge to avert my eyes. We remain like that a long moment before he puts his hand on his bulging crotch. I feel time slowing down. I stop breathing. I force myself to breathe. When I shift my gaze back to his face, he is watching me. His expression is blank. He lowers his briefs. The motion changes.

"Hell." I stand up, shrug off my bathrobe and step onto the chair. I brace my left hand against the upper window sill, in order to keep my right hand free. I use it. I let him see. He stops. He turns away and closes his curtains. I step down, put my head in my hands. Oh. I had forgotten about the plastic shower cap.

I shampoo the residual dye out of my hair, then settle in to take another bath. Many years ago I discovered that bath faucets are easy to control, in terms of temperature and intensity. The faucet handles in this apartment resemble stirrups and hold my feet well, as I maneuver into place, leaning back on my elbows.

.   .   .

"Why do they want to see fat women? Fat women are ugly," My Lover scowls. "And by the way, you're gaining weight. You look terrible. I don't know what's wrong with you." My Lover has been asked by the magazine *Venus Infers* to do a photo essay of four large women astride their enormous motorcycles wearing only helmets, gloves, and boots. "Why is it that everybody always wants me to do fat butches? Can you explain it to me?"

"No, but I don't think there's anything wrong with it, either. And by the way, I gained this ten pounds months ago, when I disappeared. You must have noticed the change before now."

"How can you say there's nothing wrong with it? *Listen to me,* Darling. The stereotype of lesbians is that they're pigs rolling around in their own slime because they can't get men. I want people to know that dykes are beautiful."

Although My Lover is good-looking—especially her Judy Davis kissable lips—at this moment she hardly looks "beautiful," despite the fact that she is unclothed.

She is wagging her finger at me as if I'd just spilled a glass of milk. Yet she's not paying me any *actual* attention; I could confess to matricide, and she wouldn't notice.

"Maybe the point is to see fat women in a different way, to change the definition of *ugly.*"

"I know all that. Don't you think I know all that? You haven't been listening to me, Darling. You don't understand anything."

"Well, didn't you tell me you liked the woman they hired as photo editor? Didn't you say she was uh, *a pleasure to work with?*"

"I don't remember." She smirks secretively.

"I think you should do it. Anyway, it could improve your rep with the lesbian community."

"I don't care what some PC-police bitches say about me."

"Of course not. Hey, do you want to go see the Andorgenie tomorrow night?"

"You're going to watch that hermaphrodite perform again? I've told you, Darling: performance art is for people who read books they don't understand. It's for people like you, who can't finish their dissertations. Do you know why there are so many female performance artists nowadays? Because females take up the tail end of every fad. The girls always play copycat, straggling after the boys."

"I never attempted a dissertation," I remind her. "And

I happen to think it's precisely *because* women have taken over performance art that everyone's so anxious to call it passé." My Lover lies back on the bed and runs her hands over her own body, clearly ignoring me. "It's that way with everything. If *women* started becoming serial sex killers, everyone would lose interest in sex killers. If more *women* became mass murderers, the public would grow bored with mass murder. If—"

"Darling, that's absurd." She reaches for my hand, presses it between her legs. "You sound utterly unbalanced."

"Well anyway, if you ever read the newspapers, you'd know that no one's been able to meet or interview the Andorgenie. You can understand why that appeals to me. I'm good at puzzles, my grandfather always said so."

My Lover extracts my hand from inside her, and pushes my fingers into my mouth. "Aren't you cute when you're ambitious. You know I could care less what you do with your free time. Darling, before you go, fix me a sandwich."

•   •   •

Another dateless night out. The Whole is now a café-theater, but it used to be an after-hours club. Two summers ago, a friend of mine worked here as a flamenco dancer. Friend, ex-friend. She probably hasn't thought of me in months, unless it was to think badly. She was completely self-centered, insufferable; dancers and singers always are. The intolerable hours I used to spend here backstage, listening to her describe her vitamin-and-exercise regimen, tagging along after her like some child trailing its mother, while she put her costume together, applied makeup, pinned up her hair. She was beautiful, beautiful. I need to calm down. Tonight I'm prepared to take risks. I have plans.

I arrive early, enter the building through a fire exit and proceed to the backstage corridor which, if I recall correctly, the two dressing rooms open onto. Hmmm. Both doors are closed. I knock on the first. It cracks open slightly, held back by a hook-and-eye. A human eye appears.

"Excuse me, I'm looking for the Andorgenie."

The door closes, then opens wide. Something smells funny.

"Want some?" she asks. I recognize her as one of the two black women from the Andorgenie's last performance. She nods her orange head toward her companion—the one with dreadlocks—sitting on a Persian carpet, in a smoking jacket. "Want some or not?"

Dreadlocks leans back against a cushion and closes her eyes while extending her hand toward me—and in it, the tip of a snaking coil of a water pipe.

"Thanks." I manage to cross the room without stumbling, sit down beside Dreadlocks, and take the pipe. All the better to win their confidence. The hash is strong. "So where is she?" I exhale smoke.

Orange-hair drops to the carpet beside me. "Why do you want to know?" She bends forward to untie her combat boots. When she pulls them off, I see a python tattoo curled around one ankle. I take another drag. Very good. So good, I have already forgotten my prepared explanation. Or, did I prepare one?

"I'd like to talk to—uh, *with*—the Andorgenie. Please."

"You mean the *and/or genie*."

"Well whatever."

"Yeah?"

"Oh you know . . . I want to interview him, or her, for an article or something. My name is Rose Anne Waldin. I'm a journalist, working for *Le Supplément*." Orange-hair looks at me blankly, then inexplicably un-zips her jeans. "Okay," I give in, "the truth is, I'd just like to meet the Andorgenie. I think we might have something in common."

Dreadlocks leans against me: "Maybe *we* have some-thing in common. Have *I* met *you* somewhere before? Where are you from?"

"New York. Manhattan," I add, in case she suspects me of being from Queens. "East Village," I lie, to be certain.

"That won't do at all," Orange-hair says.

She hands the snake's head to me again, and I oblige. We smoke in silence a while. Dreadlocks shrugs off her jacket. Oh those nipple rings.

"Excuse me. I'm sorry, but I don't understand. What's wrong with New York? What does it matter where I'm from? Where are you two from?"

"Couldn't tell you that. Hey, the clock. I have to finish getting undressed," says Orange-hair, standing up.

"You're going to be in the performance again to-night?"

"Like last time," nods Dreadlocks. "That was a dress rehearsal for tonight."

"But supposedly the Andorgenie never performs the same act twice."

"Well of course not. That would be impossible, wouldn't it? You can talk to the star in person after the show if you want, but you can't wait in here. We don't like people poking around. Come on."

They each hook an arm through mine, pull me to my feet, escort me from the room. In the corridor, one of them locks the door behind us. Then they duck through the backstage curtain and are gone. I peer through a small rip in the velvet. There's the back of the Andorgenie, standing at the podium reading from the Bible. The act has already begun.

I spread my leather coat on the floor, sit down on it

and lean against the wall. I imagine being out there on stage, performing with the lesbians. I enjoy the sound of applause. Being from a theatrical family, I'm accustomed to applause. My mother, the ambitious risk-taker, would have applauded the Andorgenie. Applause. How long have I been hearing it?

As I wrench myself from a stoned sleep, I recognize, through the applause, that broken record: "I'll be there . . . I'll be there—"

The door at the end of the corridor, through which I originally entered, opens. A few people filter through it leaving the theater. ". . . lighting had been better . . ." "Wish my girlfriend could have seen that." ". . . were sitting in the aisles." "She wouldn't recognize me." ". . . more than last time."

A cold draft reaches me. I put my arms through my coatsleeves. Silence resumes. I wait for the Andorgenie to appear. But no one does, not even the two lesbians. Then it dawns on me that I know, although I cannot exactly place, the voice that just now said, "She wouldn't recognize me."

I leap to my feet, rush down the corridor, through the door, out into the street. *Empty.* I'm too late. I return to the door, find it locked. I kick it several times, wishing I'd brought along the hatchet that Rosie stole the other day from a butcher shop. That Rosie.

. . .

"Hi, it's me."

"Where are you?" my ex-husband asks.

"Why do you want to know?"

"Are you all right?"

"Dandy schmandy. How about yourself?"

"No one's seen you for months and months. What the hell's going on?"

My throat clogs up. I sniffle into the phone.

"Look, are you sure you're all right? Why are you doing this to yourself?"

"Doing what? Doing what to myself?"

"Sweetheart, I don't have much time to talk right now, but I'm very worried about you. Let me get your phone number, I'll call you back. You know that if you need my help, you can always—Excuse me one minute." I hear muffled conversation, between him and someone else—*a woman.*

I hang up.

"Hi, it's me." I try again.

"So soon? Well, well. Couldn't wait till I got there, huh?"

"I just wanted to hear your voice."

"Uh oh. Something's not right," concludes The Bartender. "Are you being held hostage by a blind date turned maniac? Should I call the cops while you pretend to continue this conversation?" It occurs to me that The Bartender would fit in very well with my blood relatives at The House.

"I'm tired of pretending."

"Rosie, you really are not yourself. You sound weepy, gooey, and not in a good way."

"I just talked to my ex-husband."

"Whatever the fuck for?"

"I wanted to see if his voice matched one I heard the other night, that I thought I knew from somewhere."

"Was this at the theater?" asks The Bartender.

"Wait a goddamn second, how did *you* know that?"

"I knew you went because you invited me to escort you, Rosie. Remember? You invited me to 'snoop around' with you. Or did you forget I was on your B-list?"

"It was a little more like your voice," I say. The Bartender has a surprisingly soothing voice, a voice whose geniality often contradicts his words. "My memory's fuzzy. Maybe what I heard the other night was a woman's voice. I was stoned. Maybe I was imagining things. I went backstage to try to meet that Andorgenie performance artist, you know? And these two dykes who are in the show, were there, and they got me high and then they ditched me. Nothing happened, but it could have."

"Two of them at once, huh? Got you high and ditched you. Well, well. How thoughtlessly benign." Chuckling cordially, he reminds me of Captain Kangaroo. I find myself wondering whether The Bartender might, at this moment, have an erection.

"I was trying to meet the Andorgenie, to find out for myself. I got nowhere."

"Alas. But seeing me this weekend will make up for all your little disappointments."

"Alas, my ass."

"Remember, *you* called *me*." He hangs up first.

. . .

"I don't get it. One minute you're having a hundred orgasms on my tongue, and the next minute you're throwing me out."

I hand The Bartender his belt and shoes. "Don't exaggerate. It wasn't just your tongue. I was focused equally on your nose. I'm surprised you're still breathing." He frowns at me as if my glasses were crooked — but Rosie doesn't wear glasses, so I plunge blindly ahead: "I was fantasizing that you couldn't. Breathe. I mean. Well, no, actually I was fantasizing that you were my mother, and that *she* couldn't breathe. I've told you I have this compulsive fantasy about killing people, including my mother, who's well, dead. I guess that sex-and-death stuff goes back to the Greeks, huh. Slaying Medusa, and so on. Medusa being basically just a big head of female pubic hair, like Freud said. You're not the only one who reads Freud, you know. You have a good, strong nose, has anyone ever told you that?"

He nods energetically. "*Gosh* that's great, Rosie. You're a walking wound, better than television. Killing your mother, isn't that *swell.*"

"But sometimes I really do feel like killing someone."

He stoops to tie his shoes. "You can kill me some-time."

"Okay."

"Yeah, but later, not right now." He straightens up. "So, can I stay a little while?"

"Nah."

"You're going to be sorry the moment I leave."

"Wrongo. It's the moment *after* you leave that I'll be able to sit back and enjoy my regret."

"You do this too many times and it won't be cute, okay?"

"Okay—"

"Oh look, don't start crying. Listen, I'm leaving. And actually, now I *want* to leave. We've had a long couple of days together, it's a long drive home, and I have stuff to do before I go to work tonight anyway."

"What kind of stuff?"

"Not telling."

"No, really. What kind of stuff?"

"*Yes! Yes!* I've finally got your full attention!" He slings his duffel bag over his shoulder, lets himself out, and slams the door.

I wait, then sneak into the hall to watch the top of his head as he descends the stairs. I sense something underfoot: a set of keys. Medeco keys, probably the keys to his Boston apartment. Since he boasts about moonlighting as a locksmith, he won't need these anyway. But Rosie will. I tell me: *Congratulations, Double Agent X.*

·   ·   ·

I'm beginning to think The Bartender has serious intentions. He must be falling in love with me. Or with writing to me. Or with writing. Maybe because, like a lot of people, on paper he can be both sharper and blunter. I gnaw open the envelope.

Hi there, Rosie! I mean it sarcastically. We can't go on with these fucking weekends without coming to a decision. And it won't work to limit every non-sex conversation to pedantic bullshit. You live surrounded by those idiotic paintings as if you could face your fears that way, but they're just another ploy to distance yourself, to restrain your own chaos in an 'educated' framework.

You're terrified of being stupid, you're afraid there's no salvation in it. You cover up this lack of faith with a hard shell of 'intellect' but around me it has begun to crack. You worry that's insanity, but the insanity you should truly fear lies in the other direction—the catatonic numbness.

I was going to throw the I-Ching but then I realized its prudent advice wasn't what we needed so I did the tarot cards. It doesn't matter what you think of them. Someone asked a scientist about a lucky horseshoe over his door: Do you believe it works? He said no but it works even if you don't believe it. The cards gave our present situation as the hanged man, a rite of passage. Its outcome was the fool. Our only hope is to free each other's fool. I see through your hesitation. Like you, I'm afraid that if I ever give in to anyone completely, my life will be over. Well maybe it will, but not literally. Maybe only my old life will be over.

I'm sitting in a café. I'm looking at a girl I barged in on a few minutes ago in the bathroom. She didn't see me, she doesn't know I saw her with her panties down.

It was an accident. But, you know, last weekend I looked through the keyhole to watch you taking a shit. Just as I suspected, you were grimacing. Sigmund talks about how easy it is to mistake cleanliness and order for actual progress. He traces this back to our shame regarding feces. It's so humiliating to feel dirty that we forget how to love our own stench and go about denying it. 'Indeed we are not surprised by the idea of setting up the use of soap as an actual yardstick of civilization.' Are you paying attention? Having soaped up the body, we start in on the mind, trying to deodorize our thoughts and pretend we don't smell. You want to believe that by refusing to let yourself go, you can be more safely 'civilized.'

But you can't escape shit.

You talk big, Rosie, so either raise a stink or admit you're a fake. It's time for us to commit and go the distance.

By the way, I'm off to the Bahamas with Marcia for a few days. She says she misses me, she's paying for my ticket and you've got other lovers, so why shouldn't I? Let me know when you're ready to graduate grade school and play for real. I'm tired of rehearsals.

• • •

Another morning spent dozing in bed, a no-no according to my mother, who used to rouse me for kindergarten by singing, *The bright sun comes up! The dew falls away! Good morning, good morning, the little birds say!*

I open my eyes to the sound of a car alarm, and

perceive the color pink metastasizing throughout my bedroom. The bureau, rocking chair, bed frame, night table. All pink. The only large uncontaminated areas in this room are the white walls. When I shift my gaze up from the walls to my pink Chinese lantern, or down to the bed frame, I am thrown back into the nauseating pink loop.

Using all my willpower, I manage to emerge from the bed. I retreat to the wall, lean against it. Without leaving the wall, I make my way around to the window. I pull up my nightgown to press my bare breasts against the glass. Outside it is snowing, large clumps that obstinately adhere to the window sill. The idea of the snow's gradual accumulation exhausts me. I can no longer stave off the thought that in over eight months, I have accomplished virtually nothing as Rosie. Moreover, her Citibank account is almost depleted; she hasn't earned very much at her "new job," ha ha. Soon I will have to liquidate stocks under my old name, thus backsliding into a forsaken identity.

The question *Why?* is never easy. Of course I wanted to rid myself of all those hateful friends. "We're here for you. We love you," I remember them cooing after the divorce, trying to lower my guard, prodding me toward the fatal edge. But no one is going to get the better of me anymore, no.

Here I am deluding myself again. The truth is, that

most of all, I had wanted to forget my ex-husband, to avoid even hearing his name. As the months and years passed following our divorce, I would begin to feel better, then ho hum, hi ho, some friend would mention him — *Blam!* my chest would tighten, I could not breathe. If my ex-husband had abruptly died of a heart attack, I could have mourned him and recovered. But he always has been abominably healthy. I blow clouds onto the window glass, finger paint in the condensation. Crude figures emerge. I can avoid it no longer.

The thought itself is not original, but for me, the element of conviction is.

Jean Genet once hypothesized that in order to recover from having killed one person, it may be necessary to kill again. If the second murder, in turn, arouses intolerable anxiety, the antidote may be to commit a third, and so on, and so on, ad infinitum. Each homicide puts the previous ones into perspective.

My mother asked for it.

•   •   •

One fall Mom visited me at college; the following summer, I spent a few days in California. But those were the only times I saw her after she left The House, until she came to New York to visit me, and met my husband. That time, she stayed for a long weekend. She and my husband sat at our kitchen table discussing the European Economic Community, foreign films, the history of Islam, and my mother's career.

"Do you think it's natural for a woman like you to be so independent?" my husband finally challenged her.

"That word *natural* is problematic. I doubt that my own *natural* daughter even knows what the word *natural* signifies." Mom craftily turned the interrogator's spotlight onto me. "Do you, dear?" To save herself, my mother was always willing to sacrifice me.

"Okay, what does *natural* really mean?" I obediently asked.

"In ancient Greece, the word *physis*—or *nature,* as we call it in English—originally referred to the birthing process. But it was also used as the antithesis of another word, *nomos,* or *custom.*"

"Is that right," chimed my husband.

"Yes, it was biology versus culture," my mother smiled at him. "Anyway, back then, the typical Greek assumed that his own cultural customs were universal, and not at all arbitrary. But then Herodotus discovered that different customs existed in different places, the way we know today, for example, that the English shake hands whereas the Eskimos rub noses."

"Ah yes," he agreed.

"This discovery made the Greeks realize that their customs were variable, not universal at all," Mom continued. "So that word *nomos*—or *custom*—did a flip-flop and turned from connoting something nonarbitrary to connoting something arbitrary. Are you following, dear?"

"Nomos did a flip-flop," I nodded. I thought of the rubber flip-flops I had worn during family vacations at the beach. I was trying to listen.

"Now, here's what happened. Because *physis*, or *nature*, had always been the opposite of *nomos*, and now *nomos* connoted something arbitrary, suddenly *physis* began to stand for the opposite of arbitrary, that is, for inherent validity or rightness—the same qualities we still attribute to *nature* and *natural* today. But you see, this connotation has no firm basis in anything. Do you understand what I'm trying to tell you?" she asked me.

Throughout my life, I had invariably acquiesced to my mother. I had accepted without protest all the tribulations she inflicted. But now I was furious. I had reached a point of no return. I looked her in the eye and for the first time ever, I told her exactly what I thought of her arrogant oratory. "It's *hogwash*. It's *meaningless*."

She leaned toward me: "Very good! I didn't know if you were following. Which is silly, because you were always a good listener."

I loved and hated my mother so violently then, the only obvious solution was death.

It was later the same year that my mother called to tell me she had six months left to live. "I don't know if the year's half empty or half full," she said. She had often been ironic before, but seldom joked.

I flew to California the next day. "I'm moving in with you, like it or not," I declared—thus finally saying what I had always wanted to say, following my parents' divorce, some twenty years earlier. At the time, I had been too timid to speak up, and too devastated that it never occurred to Mom that I really should get out of The House. Now here she was dying in order to distance herself from me again. I guess I don't mean that *literally*. It's just that sometimes, life seems morbidly bent on repeating itself.

When I arrived at her house in Santa Monica, I arranged my clothes in the guest room as though I'd grown up there—shoving my pajamas under the pillow, color-coordinating my socks in the bureau drawer, folding my underwear into triangles, the way she'd once taught me to do dinner napkins—and I refused all her suggestions to go for a drive, take a walk on the beach, or otherwise leave home, except for necessities.

We didn't argue about it. We didn't talk, except for necessities. The TV glowed like an arctic sun, twenty-four hours. A nurse stopped by daily. My mother's friends thought she was overseas shooting a film. Being privy to the truth made me feel special, but also not;

obviously it wasn't just me she held at arm's length. I wanted to probe her with questions but succumbed to silence. As she grew weaker, we became more intimate physically—I massaged her, bathed her, dressed her—but even more distant psychically. When she told me I'd be getting some money, for a moment I thought she meant some kind of salary, as a hired hand.

One night I woke in a sweat to the realization that she was actually afraid of me, my pent-up resentments, and that I just wasn't angry at her. I was enraged. But I retreated back to sleep and by next morning could no longer admit it to myself, much less to her.

The cancer spread quickly from her stomach to her liver and beyond, but my mother never flinched. She demanded from her doctor a refillable morphine prescription. "Find out just how much it will take," she ordered me.

Relying on pharmacology textbooks at the local library, I determined it would require 200 milligrams of morphine. We had saved up 30 tablets of 15 milligrams each. "Well then, that's enough. *That's enough*," she said.

I was crying; perhaps I was happy. My mother needed me and would never leave me again for someone else. It did not last, not even six months. Within weeks, she weighed less than eighty pounds. And the cancer had lodged deep in her marrow beyond painkillers' reach. "Time to reincarnate up the corporal ladder," she announced. At her insistence, with pestle and mortar I ground up all the tablets and fed her the powder in apple juice. It was enough to kill a healthy adult more than twice her size within minutes.

My mother survived ten hours.

Throughout the night, she lay unconscious while I sat mulling her murder. She'd bow out forever while I'd be left with blood on my hands, at least morphine on my fingers. I tried sucking my thumb, it tasted bitter. I wondered whether I was getting what I most wanted, or most didn't: I was killing my mother. But I failed to wonder which would be more addictive, satisfaction or regret.

I sat staring at the wall though every now and then I peeked, I tried to watch her die. She appeared to be innocently sleeping. I knew better and probably always had. After ten hours, she made a gurgling sound, opened her blue eyes, and abruptly stopped breathing.

I sat still, held my breath. Then I tiptoed from the room, called a taxi, and packed my bag. It was morning. The hospice nurse arrived and I asked her to please take care of everything. I did say please. The taxi honked and I looked in on Mom one last time. "Bye," I said. And since it made me feel desolate, and numbly triumphant, I repeated: "Bye."

If I want to regress, I can still count those ten hours on my fingers, but I don't dwell. I try to live in the here and now, as *she* did. Although sometimes I can't resist brooding on sex and death, I try to accept the present, as *she* did. Perhaps I have failed from trying too hard.

I withdraw from the window and ease myself back into bed, mulling over various ways to die. The phone rings. I let it ring two more times, in case it is Personal Ad.

• • •

"Rosie?" It is.

"Well, well. Just didn't have the patience to wait until I called you again, did you, huh?" I hear my own voice; the act now seems inevitable.

"Hmmm . . ." Personal Ad grows silent, coughs. "You sound odd today, Rosie. I was just phoning to say I enjoyed our recent *session* together, and I'm sorry I missed your little outing last week—"

"Two weeks ago."

"—and so I thought I'd ring you up to see how it was. I do apologize about not returning your calls, I was out of town or something—"

"Or something?"

"—and so as I say, I thought I'd just give you a buzz to find out what happened."

"What do you mean, *'what happened'*?"

"I was out of town, as I just told you."

It has annoyed me before, the way Personal Ad circles

certain subjects, refusing to face them head on, circling and circling like a vulture waiting until the struggle's over. But I'm not going to be the one to surrender, not this time.

"No," I say. "I mean, why would you want to find out *what happened?* I left several messages on your machine saying that I was going to see another performance by the Andorgenie and thought you might want a second chance to go with me, having stood me up the first time. So what do you mean, *'what happened'? What happened* is that you didn't return my calls until now. As far as I'm concerned, you're totally undependable. I can't count on you to be there for me. You remind me of my mother."

"Well Rosie, considering I wore my pantyhose for you — frankly, you're being tiresome."

"As far as I'm concerned, *everything* is tiring *me*."

"I regret having called."

"No, wait. It's just —"

"Look, do you want to make plans to get together, or not?"

That's it. It is her voice.

"Yes, *yes,* absolutely. I'd like you to come over to my apartment for a goodbye dinner. Tomorrow. I'm leaving New York."

"I'm afraid I have plans for tomorrow."

"Cancel."

"What's the hurry, Rosie? What do you mean, you're leaving New York?"

"Find out tomorrow. Otherwise, you'll never know."

"My, you're difficult." Personal Ad yawns audibly into the phone. "Alright. Give me your address."

· · ·

I hang up delirious. Now there is no turning back.

The past, whose capriciousness has mesmerized me for so long, now unmasks itself as the small room in which I have spent my entire life. It is time to get out of bed. I step into a pair of panties, hook my bra, think again, remove the bra, pull on a sweater, change my mind, free my arms, put on the bra, grope for the sweater sleeves, squirm back in.

I need to be more decisive. I have spent my life in the thrall of nostalgia, self-indulgently refusing to move forward. I maneuver a deodorant bottle down through the neck of my sweater, smear a patch under each arm. It's natural to be cautious, but I've been too cautious. *Why did you refuse to move forward?* I ask myself; yet I have been moving forward all along, in spite of myself, toward the abyss. I buckle my watch strap. My head ticks. I try to calm myself, but my thoughts hurl ahead with frightening obstinacy.

"Trapped, until one day you decide to escape," I state out loud. In the kitchen, I pour coffee beans into one compartment of my electric coffee maker, and cold water into another. This amazing, high-tech machine not only grinds the beans, but filters the water. The coffee turns out so-so, but I enjoy the production. I have always wanted to keep up with the times, to know more about new gadgets than old gadgets, more about new art than old art, more about new crimes than old crimes.

"But the truth is," I vociferously admit, "a lot of things were done better in Granddaddy's day." I open a drawer, withdraw a knife, swing it back and forth until the coffee maker clicks, indicating the main phase is over. Then I throw the knife at the wall; it doesn't stick.

"Nowadays one is merely a cog in the machine. In the old days, people shot each other and got it over with." Sometimes it is best to shoot someone, get it over with, I nod, stirring half-and-half into my coffee. Oh, that's perfect: half a marriage, half a Ph.D., half a life, disappearing at age thirty-five.

"Fucking ridiculous."

Oh funny, funny, that *death,* the obvious solution, finally reveals itself as *the only way out* of my claustrophobic little, detestable little lifelong cell. The past unmasks itself as the cubicle in which I have spent my entire life—and death reveals itself as the *escape hatch.* I take one long, last swallow, then slam my empty coffee cup against the marble cutting board, breaking the cup and

cutting my finger. I smear a red X on the white marble.
Yes. Blood.

For several minutes, I force myself to sit quietly on my
living-room floor, staring at the walls, what I can see of
them. This is an exercise in self-control; the gaudy paintings threaten to avert my attention from the plain, back-
ground walls. The walls bore me, of course. Then again,
boredom can signify overstimulation: a spinning color
wheel makes us see so many colors so fast, that we can't
perceive any, but only blankness, nullity, white.

I'm confused.

I cannot decide whether the walls, or the paintings,
have pushed me to this turning point. It will be a relief
to dispose of this work.

• • •

I've decided to contact a gallery. The Totem appeals to
me because of its scandalous reputation—it was caught
last year trying to collect flood insurance on a set of
sculptures *designed* to look water-damaged—and because of its familiarity.

Familiarity can be tyrannical.

Long ago, my family used to patronize the Ponderosa
restaurant. My father's paycheck would not support any
better. My mother's taste would not support any worse.

Yet the underlying motive was one of crass *familiarity;* the Ponderosa lured my parents in like some old friend they disliked but continued to see, out of emotional lethargy. In spite of its intolerable steaks, it was an incurable habit . . . which was why my mother and I had lunch at another Ponderosa, in a different town but identical nevertheless, the time she visited me at college.

There she is, red-haired like my mother, behind the boomerang desk. It is all coming back to me, ha ha. She appears the same—pale and too perfect. She glances up, takes in my yellow latex jumpsuit, then conspicuously averts her gaze (something gallery receptionists tend to do) as if we had found ourselves alone together in a sauna. On a mat on the floor, a circle of skulls, some human, some bovine, face a gun which pivots around every few seconds and shoots out ocher-colored liquid, each time hitting one of the skulls in the face. I myself would give this piece a bad review.

"Hey," I call to the Totem's proprietor. "Nobody's buying this stuff, are they?"

"Excuse me?"

"Money. Nobody's dishing it out lately. Why do you think that is?"

"Excuse me, have we met?"

"My name's Rose Anne Waldin. I'm working on a piece for *Le Supplément.*"

"Oh, well why didn't you say—"

"And listen, I could put together a show for you that I know would sell."

"I see. So you don't really work for *Le Supplément*. You're free to send us your slides but we're not in a position to take on new talent just now."

"I'm not here to talk about my own work anyway. This is about somebody already famous. I own twenty John Wayne Gacy paintings."

"*Gacy.*"

"Yeah, you know—while on death row, he did oil paintings and sold them from prison by mail order. I own all the works from what I call his color-by-number period, as well as a series of self-portraits done around the time his circuit-court appeal got rejected. These are very emotional, very evocative paintings."

"I see," she says. "I'm sorry, the idea makes me queasy."

Until now, I have shared my Gacy collection with The Bartender and no one else, not even My Lover. She projects an image of open-minded tolerance, but is secretly terrified of the unexpected. My Lover cannot endure those exceptional moments when I appear to be *smarter* than she. I am not allowed even to speak in the same *tone* she does.

I don't believe this woman's hair color is natural. It

may be a wig. I could snatch it off her head; that might teach her. Older women invariably expect younger women to kowtow to them. Older lesbians are the worst, although the best in bed, of course. This woman probably wants me to flatter her.

"Oh come on, give Gacy a chance. After all, David Letterman owns one of his paintings. You like David Letterman, don't you? And besides, just look at these skulls. *They* make *me* queasy."

"My dear," huffs the redhead. "This circle of skulls conveys a refreshing pessimism, after the glibness of eighties theory. It refutes Baudrillard's notion of life being escaped through death. This piece implies we're forever trapped in a vicious circle, where God is dead but still pissing on us." She smiles serenely. "A refreshing pissimism."

Her jocularity fails to unsettle me. "I think you'll find Gacy's work challenging. It puts a brand new gloss on notions of *appropriation* and *simulacrum*."

Finally, my graduate studies may bear fruit. The education cost a great deal. That intellectual stimulation deepened and intensified until it swept like a tidal wave through my marriage. Initially, it was *graduate school* that made me lust after all sorts of knowledge. How could I finish my studies, when my studies had finished my marriage? I could not. I would not. I refused.

"I'm afraid that those warm, fuzzy postmodern theories tend to sound a bit forced these days, or even—with all due respect, dear—to sound naive."

I reach for the glass paperweight on her desk, shift it from hand to hand. "Don't call me 'dear.' *Pretty please.* Let me explain. Sherrie Levine does those pictures of Krazy Kat, right? And David Salle recycles movie stills and famous photos and stuff. Okay, well *Gacy* was ahead of his time. He painted the Seven Dwarfs, Bambi, Pinnochio, and so on, but he painted them *even more badly* than the Disney pictures he copied. And this, this *refreshing excrescence* stands out in the paintings I happen to own."

She appears to be listening, so I talk faster: "You see, these works push that whole blurring-boundaries thing to outer limits. And then, in the portraits, Gacy painted himself dressed up as Pogo the Clown. Just think of the self-portraitist Pogo the Clown slaughtering all those boys. If someone could act the part of a clown, while actually committing murder, why couldn't someone else *act the part of a murderer, while actually*—"

"What's your point?"

"Look, David Salle says his own works are dead—

Hah! These paintings are more up to date because they're *much, much more dead*. And Gacy himself was executed for being America's most proficient serial killer. We're talking about a limited supply. Death sells, but this is murder. That's gotta sell."

"I'm sorry. I don't think I could market them."

"Anyway look," I plead, "In the future just try to remember that *my* Gacy collection is special."

She opens a book and bends over it as if reading. She wants me to leave. I obligingly head for the door.

"If you don't return that paperweight to my desk immediately, I will activate the alarm system."

I stop and turn toward her again. The paperweight is the size of a baseball, but heavier and harder, made of evil green glass. I raise it in both hands as if preparing to pitch. Suddenly there's a terrible noise. It continues ringing as I walk toward her; the police are always too slow and will never catch me.

"I was just pretending!" I yell over the alarm. I set the paperweight on her desk and hurry out, calling to her over my shoulder, "I like to pretend!"

I should have known better than to look back. While doing so, I catch my high heel on the raised ledge of the door frame, and fall to the sidewalk, badly bruising my thigh.

• • •

Well, that round's over.

Buoyed by the auspicious start of my new career, I decide not to order out for Chinese food after all. That night five months ago when Personal Ad and I first met, she asked me to cook for her sometime. Okay. I will do it tonight. She knows nothing about my plans, of course. Like everyone else, she has suffered from the illusion that she understands me.

Years ago, my therapist told me, "You have a childish belief in openness and honesty, a naive faith in confession and forgiveness."

She was right, they always are. Since then, I have learned to tell lies and keep secrets, even from curious types like Personal Ad. I'm . . . *smart* now. Got it? There is something funny about secrets, however. It turns out that the more secrets I accumulate of my own, the more I want to uncover *other people's* secrets. My *own* secretive privacy often causes me unbearable anxiety, and I have found that this can be alleviated only by invading *others'* secret domains.

"And those walls come a-tumbl-in' down," I sing off-key, setting out for the grocery store.

Sometimes the mere thought of shopping for groceries disheartens me, but not now. Groceries, ho! Like John Wayne striding into a saloon, I throw back the

Korean grocer's plastic-flap doorway and stare down the other customers. They wilt and scatter. Usually, they intimidate me. Usually my only hope is for some misfit to appear, a derelict, say, or a paraplegic, who will distract the other shoppers' hostile attention. But not now. As coolly as John Wayne pulling in his poker winnings, I sweep items into a basket: limes, tomatoes, onions . . . I draw my wallet as swiftly as my Colt .45, pay without even needing change, then onward to the butcher's for a duck. Rosie stole the hatchet, but she'll pay for the duck. A duck would be mighty fancy, oh yes.

I feel good. I so rarely feel good. I am in control. I am planning dinner. It's not that I have anything against Personal Ad. It doesn't bother me to waste my time thinking over her family history, what she has gone through, her Ph.D., or the book she is writing. The fact that I have wasted endless time comparing her to myself, ad nauseam, has never bothered me.

"But we have reached the point," I tell the duck, lying on bloody wax paper atop my cutting board, "that we have to act, you understand? Yes, quack quack."

● ● ●

Personal Ad is shorter in my apartment than she was in hers. Because my ceiling is higher and because she is craning her neck backward, looking up.

"What . . . What are all these?"

"Those? Oh those. Those are just artwork. Don't waste your time staring. I'm getting rid of those paintings very soon. They sort of came with the apartment."

"Did they. Well then." Personal Ad lowers herself delicately into the rocking chair, which I have moved into the living room from the bedroom, since I never got around to buying new furniture. I give Personal Ad a paper cup to use as an ashtray. She looks lovely, in pleated wool slacks, and the same sweater she had on last time; how endearingly familiar. Something is wrong. She surveys the lower half of the room, avoids eye contact.

"So. Is it all just the way you found it, here? I mean, are you planning to . . . ? Not that there's anything wrong with your ah, wall hangings or, or a pink TV stand . . . or even the pink TV itself. There's nothing wrong with that. Although I am a bit, ah . . . It's just that this isn't what I had imagined when you . . . No, I, well I . . . Well! I'm afraid I can only stay a few minutes. I was unable to cancel my plans. You remember, Rosie, I said I had plans." She squints as if smiling, takes a long pull on her cigarette.

"I'm sure you did. At least stay for a drink. Here." I hand her the glass. She recoils slightly, then accepts.

While doing pharmaceutical research for my mother years ago, I happened across the fact that sodium amytal,

{157}

primary ingredient of my sleeping pills, is also the truth serum preferred by detectives. Through experimentation, I determined that it is rendered virtually tasteless when mixed with lime and pineapple juice.

"The TV was a frivolous afterthought," I assure Personal Ad. "I had extra paint."

"That means . . . so you did do this all . . . yourself."

"Oh yes, I like doing things myself." I wheel my desk chair closer to her and sit down. "Don't worry. Pink's not really my favorite color either."

"No. Well." Personal Ad shakes her naturally blonde head and quickly finishes her drink.

It has been interesting playing Double Agent X, but one gets tired of watching oneself. Voyeurism is more pleasurable when it entails spying on *others,* particularly specimens as reserved as Personal Ad. How satisfying it was, once upon a time, to see tabloid photos of Princess Di, caught unawares without her bikini. Subsequently toppled from Her Royal Highness's pedestal, she commanded less attention, of course . . . until death resurrected her. Some people are simply more attractive dead. Personal Ad resembles Princess Di. Alas, she too has fallen in my regard, and I am no longer cowed by her regal detachment.

I lacked the courage to confront my mother before she died, to ask her point blank why she kept such distance between us. *Just what was she hiding, what secret game was she playing that she feared I would discover?* If I had known that, I might not have felt like some leper she had abandoned, cut off from civilization. Even the *pets* grew uncivilized, after Mom left. The dog and cat both took to urinating on the beds in The House. Maybe they'd lost all sense of orientation, because soon they both got run over, so terribly mauled we put them to sleep. I never found courage to ask Mom whether she missed the pets, much less me. I still miss the pets. Someday I will get another pet, but it won't be the same. You lose one chance, you get another, but it is never the same.

Tonight I won't miss my chance. Why, tonight if Satan himself made the perfect pitch, I would acquiesce. My curiosity about Personal Ad has mounted to the point where there's no choice; I *must* give in. Oh giddy, giddy.

I pour her another drink. Tomorrow she will likely remember nothing. It takes a few minutes for the sodium amytal to kick in, so I have time to draw her out. "It should be almonds or cashews instead, huh?" I ask, handing her the tray of guacamole and chips.

"Beg your pardon?"

"We should be having some kind of nuts, shouldn't we?" I say amiably. "After all, we *are* some kind of nuts, aren't we? You and I?"

She glowers silently.

"Let me ask you this: Would you think I was daffy if I told you I had killed someone and was planning to do it again? Oh please, obviously I'm only joking!"

She gapes at me. The drug has perhaps destroyed her sense of humor.

"Seriously now, there's something I've been meaning to ask you, about yourself."

"Hmmm?" At last, Personal Ad smiles woozily.

"You've got some pretty big secrets, haven't you?"

"What?"

"Alright, you do some performing on the side, don't you?"

"Some what?"

I drain my glass. I had not wanted to come right out and confront her, because it was more fun to play cat and mouse. But I am suddenly very tired. Exhausted. I slowly, deliberately, rise to my feet like Perry Mason rising from the defense table for the clincher. I plant myself directly before the witness whose noose of lies I am prepared to draw tight. Weary from my long years of experience, my accumulated knowledge of human improbity, I face her with joyless determination.

"Are you not now, and in fact, haven't you been for indeed quite some time, a performance artist who goes by the stage name of 'Andorgenie'? Haven't you, in fact, been leading a life of subterfuge and multiple identities?

Isn't it true that all this talk of employment in the insurance industry, all this talk about writing some book, all of this talk is just a coverup, just a smoke screen—"

"My God, you are deranged, aren't you? I always knew you projected a lot, but now I see you really are psychotic! Where's my purse?" Personal Ad looks around wildly, snatches her purse strap from around the arm of the rocking chair, and leaps to her feet, sending the chair into paroxysms. Rocking so fast it blurs into a pink mist. With a floating yet sinking feeling, I realize I drank from the wrong glass. As Personal Ad lunges toward the door, an unnatural desire to tell the whole truth overwhelms me.

"Your voice, it sounded so familiar. It seemed uncanny. Then you had that vibrator. And the Andorgenie had all those vibrators. Everything seemed to fit together. You never were available on the nights of the performances. Sometimes you imitated my voice. You liked to role-play in bed. I felt you always kept a wall between us. I thought if you were the Andorgenie, it would explain everything. The more I fantasized about it, the more real it seemed, the more certain of it I became. Nothing made sense, otherwise—"

I hear my voice cracking inappropriately, reminding me of my brother.

"—why you were so standoffish toward me sometimes, and how you could be doing so well after that stuff with your uncle. That should have made you insane or at least a drug addict, certainly not a Ph.D. I mean—"

Nothing is turning out as planned.

"—why should you be allowed to air your problems, while I . . . I hated thinking about you. I wanted *you* to be thinking about *me*. You seemed to have some secret formula that you wouldn't let me in on. I thought you held the key. I thought I'd stop being tormented by questions, all the time questions, more questions, the sound of your voice—"

I stop because there is no sound of her voice, only the sound of her shoes descending the stairs, which I hear quite clearly through the open door.

•   •   •

I awake on the living-room floor, still dressed. *Daylight*. More footsteps on the stairs. I see the door is still open, was apparently never closed. Personal Ad will forgive me, allow me to explain. After all, she is a kind person, a good person. Or maybe not.

I stagger to my feet. The crippling remorse begins to dissipate. There is always a second chance (even if it's never the same). I remove my parched contact lenses, eye myself in the bathroom mirror, then linger with face upturned under the hot shower. My brother takes six-hour baths, as I recall. Into the kitchen for some hot coffee, so what if it is mediocre. While waiting for my coffee machine's final *click,* I check the oven dial; yes, I remembered last night to switch off the gas. I crack the door, peer in at the duck, forlorn and pallid on the rack of a blood-puddled roasting pan. Ah. I never remembered to turn *on* the oven. "We're not cooked yet," I console the bird, slamming the oven shut.

Okay, so my brother "is" God.

I study my face in the toaster. I do not resemble him, except for the black hair. But I too have yearned for some grand solution, some master answer. *Making oneself into God,* "the mother of all answers," I laugh. The sound frightens me. Then I remember to close the front door, which Personal Ad thoughtlessly left open.

I turn up the radio for the weather. I don't like to drive in the rain. I don't like how Personal Ad left everything hanging. At our final session three years ago, my therapist warned me of the importance of "closure."

She made it sound as if I could simply close one book and open another. But in my experience, we have only one Book of Life, as Leibniz said. The author is God and God is dead, but still . . . Oh I suppose that Totem woman knew a few things.

The radio calls today "a sunny Wednesday." So that's why I'm up and about so early: I slept through yesterday. Hi ho. After a few phone calls, I'll rent a van and drive my Gacy paintings over to PostWorld. I'll tell them to deliver the paintings C.O.D. to the Totem Gallery after a few days. The gallery owner didn't want to deal with Gacy and me, but soon she may change her mind.

She can't be forced to pay up—but if all works out, people will *believe* that Rose Anne Waldin has made a real killing. And that's what counts. After PostWorld, I'll stop at the butcher's for the goods I've ordered, and then at Citibank, to withdraw Rosie's last seven hundred dollars, enough to take The Bartender on a smashing Christmas holiday.

· · ·

Rosie or not, I've always looked forward to the Christmas season.

When I was a girl, we would drive from Ohio to New York to visit my grandfather for the holidays. It was the only time that my brother resembled a normal child, that his glasses were neither askew nor taped together, that his shirt was neither stained nor inside out, that he said or did appropriate things, and that whenever he tried to smile, he actually smiled. As soon as the holidays ended, however, my brother reverted to abnormality.

All those years, my parents refused to acknowledge his condition, or their own. They assumed the best. Now, to *consciously* fantasize about something can be helpful. But to live inside a fantasy without realizing it, is invariably catastrophic. Probably the reason I cannot remember much from those days is that a fog of impending catastrophe permeated our existence—indeed, at least one of us was almost always bedridden with some flu or headache—and this pall lifted only during conversations about Granddaddy, or Christmas trips to see Granddaddy.

En route from our Ohio home to Granddaddy's New York penthouse, Mom led car games. When it grew dark, Dad told ghost stories. Sometimes nothing lifts my spirits so much as driving all day and night by car. My brother's doctors should try prescribing long car rides, instead of Prolixin Deconate, Cogentin, and Mellaril— although the injections and pills do make him less of a Hannibal Lecter type, more of a Howdy Doody type, from what I can gauge on the telephone. Until now, long car rides have always cured me. Because I am going somewhere, as they say, *in the driver's seat,* as they say. Every so often I pull off Interstate 95 to reread The Bartender's last letter:

I see through your hesitation.

Oh yeah?

The insanity you should truly fear lies in the other direction— the catatonic numbness.

He might be more pleasant if he were a little more catatonic himself.

It's time for us to commit.

Some people who fall in love prefer to chain themselves to the source of their trouble. There are others whose inclination is to get as fast and far away as possible from the so-called love object. But often the only way out is to . . . Pink has failed me.

Like you, I'm afraid that if I ever give in to anyone completely, my life will be over. Well maybe it will, but not literally. Maybe only my old life will be over.

The Bartender is wrong; *I* am not afraid of anything. Yet he is right about his old life. That was his idea, anyway. But of course, most of the scheme is mine. After all, *he's* so old-fashioned, he *hand-writes* his letters. I'm so technologically advanced, I never do anything by hand. Even now, I've got my laptop with me.

I'm off to the Bahamas with Marcia. . . . you've got other lovers, so why shouldn't I?

He may be logically correct, but who cares. Marcia can't be very interesting. A few days with her will pale in comparison to what's in store for us. Yet I wonder what to do with The Bartender when it's all over. Except for My Lover, relationships tend to die on me quickly, and then it's pointless to haul around the dead weight.

Men can be difficult to dispose of. Although I've avoided seeing my father and brother for almost two decades, insidious fragments reemerge, settling and un-settling, like bats.

But people change, and any moment could be a turning point. Friends turn into enemies; the living into the dead; victims into victimizers. Maybe it's all immanently predictable. How pathetic that we all want to be unpredictably *original*. We all want to be *God* instead of jellyfish. The Bartender and I think we're oh-so-clever, but perhaps we are merely players on a stage, destined to act out someone else's script.

That's not original.

. . .

"Freeze."

"Shit! Jesus, what are you doing here? Be careful!"

"No, Big Boy. *You* be careful. Like I said, *freeze.* That means don't move, just like on TV. This is all going to be just like on TV, except it'll be real. You move once more I'll blow your fucking head off. See, it sounds almost like TV, but it's real, get it?"

"Okay, okay, I got it. Rosie, is that gun . . . ?"

"Is it *what?* Is it *loaded?* Is it duh, *deadly?* Is it pointed at you? What do you think?"

"I don't know. I don't know you as well as I thought I did. How did you get in?"

"Listen to you: *I don't know you as well as I thought I did.* Bet you wish one of your other girlfriends were here now, eh? Bet you know them pretty well."

"Uh—"

"You don't know me, but I have the keys to you. Or at least, to your place. Okay Babycakes, thaw out enough to put one foot in front of the other until you reach that little spot I've made for you to sit over there, on that piece of plastic beside the radiator."

"I'll do anything you say, just please—Here?"

"That's right, now sit down facing me, relax and take your shoes off."

"It's hard to relax with that gun—"

"I *said* take your fucking shoes off."

"Right."

"*Right.* Now, I want you to take your pants off . . . Very gooood. Now see that pair of open handcuffs there? I want you to handcuff one of your ankles to the radiator pipe."

"Oh God."

"Be sure to stay on the plastic."

"The plastic—"

"*Right,* the plastic. Now close the handcuffs until they click. I've got to hear those two clicks . . . Gooood. Lean away from your ankle so I can walk around you to check the cuffs . . . Good boy. That's smart of you not to try anything foolish. They can be foolish on TV because good guys don't get killed on TV, unless they're fat. Since you've become so attached to the radiator, I might as well tell you that the plastic is a zip-lock body bag, the disposable kind."

{168}

"It's one of my mother's dress covers!"

"It works the same way. You've been a very good boy, and now we're going to give you a treat."

"Oh Jesus."

"I'm going to throw something at you and I want you to catch it. Here."

"Hey, this is—hey—"

"Yes, of course, it's *yours*. I found it in the bag with the rest of them under your bed. I've been here a while. I looked around and made myself at home, like Goldilocks. And now you're going to give me something for the porridge, my big bear. Don't look so glum. I said don't—"

"Just please stop waving that thing at me, it might go off."

"Smile! I want you to give yourself a hard-on."

"If I can't—"

"Oh but you can! And you can start by putting that little dildo right up your you-know-what."

"But that'll hurt."

"Now, now, I think we've done it before, haven't we? What were so many of them doing under your bed?"

"Well, women like—"

"*Don't tell me what women like.* It's clean, I washed it for you. Gooood boy! Come on now, up the little tunnel. Very very good! You look ravishing. Okay, that's enough."

"Owwh."

"Well, there we go—half hard already! Now, see what I've got waiting for you, a bowl of fresh strawberries with sugar on them. Once you produce that *crème fraîche,* you're all set with your just dessert."

"I don't even like straw—"

"*Shut up.* They aren't for you. They're for the police, like leaving a plate of cookies for Santa. You should be glad I'm giving you a *Good Housekeeping* kind of send-off. What a way to go, eh? Maybe this isn't like TV after all, Big Bear. Maybe it's *better."*

. . .

BOSTON (AP)—In answer to a 911 call, police this morning entered an apartment near North Station to find the blood-soaked scene of a sex killing—and signs that the killer had absconded moments earlier with the corpse of her male victim.

By press time, investigators had begun to piece together a scenario described as "horrifying." Apparently, the victim—a 34-year-old man whose name is withheld pending notification of kin—was slain by a sex-crazed girlfriend so enraged by jealousy that she tape-recorded the attack, police sources said.

Among various pieces of evidence were the audio recording and a gallon of blood in the bathtub, ac-

cording to one source. "From the tape it's apparent that she cut him up before forcing him into the tub, where she shot him. No one could sustain that much blood loss and live."

Police said they identified the victim through personal documents found in his home, but by press time had not yet identified a suspect.

An anonymous call to 911 just after midnight reported loud thumping in the back stairwell, following yelling and gunfire from the fourth floor of the Merrimac Street building. Officers arrived to find the victim's door open and his apartment ransacked and blood-smeared. They also found a bloody hatchet and "various sexual torture devices," said police spokesman Sean McDonnel.

Blood samples were taken from the apartment as well as from an outside hall, a back stairway, and an alley behind the building—evidence that the corpse had been dragged to a getaway vehicle, possibly only moments before police arrived.

"It's all pretty horrifying," McDonnel said.

Police found the perpetrator's mini-cassette tape inside a folded newspaper, according to one source. "There was a Tampax, a twenty-dollar bill, bobby pins, and a tube of lipstick too. It's possible her purse spilled open and she didn't even realize it. On the tape, it sounds like she's not quite all there."

The source added that the attacker—raving with jealousy over another woman—sadistically taunted her victim while forcing him to perform lewd acts, before apparently slaying him in a sexual frenzy.

She also destroyed bloodstain patterns inside the apartment that might have given investigators valuable information, one officer said off-record. "The stains in the stairwell are untouched. There you can see the body was dragged. Inside, we've got blood on the walls, floor, refrigerator, everywhere, but it has all been wiped over."

The officer noted that this would be the Boston Police Department's first sex murder in which the killer was female and the victim male.

. . .

"I'm proud of you, Miss Killer. How do you feel?"

"Very happy with myself."

"Good." She finger-paints baby oil, loop-de-looping across my skin. I don't usually lie to My Lover. In fact I'm not very happy with myself. I feel guilty about The Bartender. Despite my own behavior these last many years, deep down I have remained secretly mistrustful of nonmonogamy. Betrayal's tricky. It looks like freedom but can about-face and become self-entrapment. Then again—

"What are you thinking, Darling?"

"There's nothing that can't be reversed. One can always reflip-flop."

"Flip-flops do come in pairs."

She doesn't really care what I was thinking. She never takes me seriously. I'm a toddler putting on a little play.

"The fun's not over yet," I warn her.

"No, it's really never over with you."

"So we're still—?"

"Why not? Although to be safe, you shouldn't contact me for a while. I hope you appreciate my staying mum." I suppose. Though it has long annoyed me that My Lover lacks any firm moral principles. "It would be so much simpler to turn you in."

"To what?" I ask, rolling onto my stomach, winding her raw-silk bedspread around me. I want her to dissuade me from going away. I want her to cling with warm, tender anxiety. She gives me a brisk shove, unrolling and reexposing me.

"Don't be broody, Darling. You think I'm unemotional, but that's because I'm objective. For me, life consists of story problems—multiplying two negatives to get a positive, and so forth. *No* may equal *no,* but a *no-no* is a plus." She daubs more oil from nipple to bellybutton. "Your caper far outshines that sexually confused performance artist."

"There's something else I haven't told you—"

"Shhhh." She paints my mouth shut. "*Oh don't we*

{173}

make an awful mess, when we endeavor to confess. You'll miss my erudition."

"Your quick tongue. I'll be back."

Of course I will. My Lover is the opposite of my ex-husband. She will never tell me to leave — or stay. She imprisons me in endless tolerance.

"Hold still. Knees up please. What's this on your thigh?"

"Bruise," I say, remembering the fall.

"I realize that."

"Look, I'm involved in something serious — "

"Stop being ridiculous." My Lover slips a pacifier between my lips, exits the room, and returns. She sets a tray on the bed, then kneels on the rug.

"Scissors."

I obediently hand her scissors from the tray. I feel my pubic hair repeatedly tugged and released as she crops it short. I hear the slosh of water, sense the tingle of a warm wet brush lathering shaving cream between my legs.

"Razor." She works silently, *carefully.* "New razor." It gently scrapes against me. "Beautiful," she announces. "Goo goo ga ga. Now, let's dust your bum."

"I like the smell of that baby powder," I teethe.

"Hush." She presses a pillow over my face. "Don't move until I get back."

At least *she* is enjoying this. The longer I lie here alone waiting, the smaller and sillier I feel. My, what soft, bald skin I have around my little red riding hood.

"Ow!" My hand was slapped.

"It's not nice to touch yourself. Dada will do that."

The pillow slides off, nudged aside by something cold against my throat—the toe of a jackboot. I see My Lover is also wearing her sideburns, mustache, military jacket, and pipe.

• • •

BOSTON (AP)—What had looked like Boston's first-ever female-sex-killer case became shrouded in mystery yesterday as police named a suspect but otherwise suppressed new information.

The unusual hush-up came less than 24 hours after police entered the home of a 34-year-old male to find his apartment awash in the blood of his apparent murder.

Even longtime sources turned reticent about a case described earlier yesterday morning as "horrifying." One did say, however, that certain unspecified details have baffled investigators. "We're not sure what we've got. It may not be homicide. It could be a kidnapping, so we have to be circumspect."

Long-distance phone records and an anonymous

tip led Boston police to identify New Yorker Rose Anne Waldin, 36, as the suspect, said department spokesman Sean McDonnel. Local police dispatched to her Manhattan apartment found it vacated. No biographical information was available by press time on Waldin, who allegedly left behind a tape recording of the sexually motivated attack. A warrant has been issued for her arrest.

"We're asking that anybody who knows her, or her whereabouts, please contact the police," McDonnel said.

He refused to confirm or deny that Boston Police Chief John O'Hara had imposed a gag order on officers.

• • •

I was speed-reading that article for days without slowing down. Time sure flies when you're on the run. We're jolly drunk. What's round on the ends and high in the middle? A dildo with balls, or *Ohio*. Ho, ho, ho.

But now here we are snowed in, in the Motor Inn, next to a Wal-mart, off Interstate 70. Outside, it's sixteen degrees Fahrenheit and sleeting across monotonous miles of flat farmland. Chin up! Because inside, by gum, we've a bottle of rum, daisy wallpaper, and a bouncy bed. I'm "Jane Doe" here, safe but bored (a common dilemma), patiently waiting for the sleet to stop.

I should have been more patient with Personal Ad. Curiosity compelled me to pounce — just as my long-ago cat could never resist pouncing on whatever moved beneath the bedspread, even if it was my hand she sank her fangs into, the same hand that then emerged to fling her off the bed — *Whap!* onto the floor, casting her away just as I myself have repeatedly been cast away. Oh kitty, kitty.

I keep calling Personal Ad. "Look, I need to talk to you. I can explain everything," I tell her machine.

There is not much to do here, so my ducky and I spend hours in the bath, drinking and singing along with carols on the radio. My favorite is "Jingle Bells," because I know most of the words. "Laughing all the way! Ha ha ha!" and so on. He either doesn't have a favorite or won't admit to one.

. . .

BOSTON (AP) — The blue wall of silence surrounding Boston's so-called Fatal Femme case began to crack yesterday when a source revealed to the Associated Press that blood samples taken from the crime scene have proved to be nonhuman.

Forensic hematologists determined that the samples "are all from the Anatidae family, in other words waterfowl, apparently domestic duck," the source told AP.

It was not immediately clear what this discovery

means in a case garnering national attention for its grisly scenario of a jealous woman wreaking sexual violence against a man.

Police yesterday continued to search for New Yorker Rose Anne Waldin, 36, and her possible victim, a 34-year-old Bostonian whose name is being withheld. Authorities were still trying to contact his mother, a businesswoman currently traveling in Indonesia, AP has learned.

Meanwhile in New York, a Soho art gallery released a statement asserting familiarity with the suspect, about whom little information has surfaced.

"Before becoming a fugitive, Rose Anne Waldin consigned to the Totem Gallery a number of oil paintings by the late serial murderer John Wayne Gacy, all of which Ms. Waldin has co-signed on the front in pink acrylic with her own signature. These paintings are available for viewing and sale to serious collectors by appointment only. Under the circumstances, we believe that Ms. Waldin's collection is special."

Contacted by phone, gallery owner Susan Morgan said the Totem possesses documentation verifying Waldin's signature—including her driver's license and Social Security card—and is "fully cooperating" with police. Morgan declined further comment.

Gacy was executed in May 1994 for the slaughter of 33 young men and boys. During his 14 years in a Menard, Ill., prison, he sold paintings by mail order, and was also at times represented by art dealer Rick Staton, a mass-murder enthusiast.

· · ·

The snow has finally stopped. So we can resume our journey, onto the interstate, over the river and through the woods, toward The House. No more slothful hours spent drinking, bathing, or lying in bed with my laptop, rereading the World Wide Web edition of *Le Supplément*.

[Editor's Note: The following letter was electronically transmitted to our office from fugitive Rose Anne Waldin, who has written unsigned performance-art reviews for this paper since last April. Because a warrant was issued for Ms. Waldin's arrest, we have notified authorities of this column's transmission. We refused, however, to withhold it from publication. Our decision is not meant to condone physical violence of any sort.]

Dear Readers including the police,

Industrious and repetitive as psycho killers invariably are—well! I'm a busy little bee flying around circles. Did I say 'in'? Buzz, buzz, avoiding the bumbling fuzz, who'll never know who I am. Did I say 'was'?

Stick with me, Honey, I'm just your typical word-processor-turned-sex-killer. You probably wonder what childhood abuse made me a demonic maniac. It's true that, like Charlie Manson and Henry Lee Lucas, I was forced to wear dresses to grade school.

And so some years ago, my evil nature began to assert itself. Fantasies of death and murder snuck into my thoughts, eventually invading my entire being. By that time, I was in graduate school and knew what to do. I went to the library.

I learned I was not alone. Many other sensitive, educated people felt as I did. But nobody as yet had formed a support group, and reading about the others made me feel small.

Because these Great Men weren't just thinking, they were actually killing for pleasure! They risked lives (albeit others') for their ideal, and some of them got booked. They languish in jail today, Heroic types we might well compare with the bookish de Sade.

Yes, all were men and many considered themselves artists, such as John Wayne Gacy, whose mail-order paintings were an inspiration, almost worth the $25 apiece I paid. After years of procrastination, it turned time for me to act.

I have one regret, dear readers: the fact that I'm bidding adieu without having first tracked down the Andorgenie. As your columnist, I did try, but I failed.

Maybe I didn't try too hard. And maybe that's for the best. It's natural to want to know everything, to tie all the loose ends together. But just because it's *natural* doesn't mean it's *smart*. Last night I stopped dreaming of total knowledge, and it dawned on me:

The Andorgenie, dear readers, is not *one* person pretending to be *several* people, but *several* people pretending to be *one* person. Various performers have been taking turns at playing the same part, or rather *different parts* under the *same name,* the "Andorgenie."

Probably Juan Rescate is off in Mexico, visiting long-lost relatives until the time is right to resurrect himself.

Oh these artists have been making fools of us. As they will always be wont to do. And don't we love them? Because now and then, everyone needs to be made a fool of—or else we end up fooling ourselves.

Obvious, isn't it? But sometimes the obvious escapes us.

I'm afraid this is it, dear readers. Ta da! Excuse me: Ta ta.

.   .   .

Once I saw through the Andorgenie, I saw through myself. I always knew I was just one person among many. Now I see I'm also many, vainly trying to add up to one. I've been frantically ramming the puzzled pieces together, in hopes of some perfect self, memory, image, or even *family,* as if all my irreconcilable relations could lock into one happy whole.

No wonder we're so tired.

"I remember our first night here."

"Oh yeah?"

"Well not *here.* I mean inside the car. My head was right there, where you're putting that suitcase—" I point over his shoulder, "against the tire hump."

"Let's hope you're not indulging in any gooey romantic sentimentality about us." The Bartender withdraws from the station wagon, admires his packing arrangement and rubs his hands: *finished.*

I stamp the motel-parking-lot slush off my duck boots. "I thought you liked me, Ducky Wucky."

"I'm here, aren't I?"

Men are known to mistake their mere presence for heroism. "You're just coming along for the ride," I remind him.

"It's not only that you're paying me. It's curiosity."

"Don't expect to be satisfied."

"Get in the car."

"How rude. Your mother spoiled you."

"You're right, and this is her car. *Isn't it.* Get in." He looks unhealthy despite his Bahamas tan.

I shake my head: "*I'd* like to drive. *I* know which roads to take from here."

I don't, in fact, but as usual lying works. I settle into the driver's seat, start the engine. A cold morning. The Bartender dons a corduroy jacket over his wool sweater, then pulls on his huge black coat. His face looks puny and bug-eyed behind his glasses. If he weren't attractive, he would be repulsive.

Over the last few days, we've learned to loathe each other: banal interactions—*Hand me the toothpaste, Here you go, Thank you*—quiver with animosity. We mercilessly scrutinize one another, searching for faults, as if we had a *relationship*. Which we don't. We've grasped the old knives stuck in each other's backs—and twisted them all. We've taken terrible pleasure in pushing each other to the edge, pushing again, more, again, more, until we fall, hopeless, into the abyss, into each other's grasp, *Bye-byeee*.

"I'm glad you're here," I say doubtfully. He looks out his window.

Well at least killing The Bartender has turned out better than killing my mother. For me, fantasy often surpasses reality.

The power of projection is enormous, of course.

"What were those women's clothes doing in your bedroom?"

"My mother's company makes clothing. As you already know. She owns the building where I live. As you

{183}

already know. Sometimes she stores stuff there. As you already know. So, as—"

"Yeah, yeah, Mom's an explanation for everything."

"I think we're warmed up now."

"Thank you for changing the subject." I back us out of the parking space.

"Where are the saltines?"

"Back there."

He turns around, leans over the seat. If I floored the gas pedal, he would fly over and fatally hit his head on his metal suitcase.

"Don't forget to put on your seat belt," I whisper.

I imagine his feet floating slow-motion past me en route to doom. One winter I watched an Olympic skier break her neck over and over, on TV. I didn't want to watch, but then I did. Anytime now, Fox Television's New York office will receive the crate Rosie sent. Bomb squad or not, they'll keep the cameras whirring as the body bag opens to reveal the mannequin, its hand on its crotch. Caught in the act.

The Bartender rummages through the saltines, a nauseating habit. Last year My Lover unwrapped every one of my Valentine's chocolates before choosing.

"What is this? What's the wig doing in the saltine box?"

"That's definitely a tin, not a box. The original wig is

on the Rosie dummy where we put it. This is a *new* one just like it."

"Why should I think you're not lying?"

"Hopefully you'll see it on TV."

"A *souvenir*. How thoughtful."

"I figured you'd want something to remember me by. That wig's my signature."

I knock him off balance a second, veering to the right, following signs for the Columbus Airport. I'll deposit him and the car in the parking garage. For his own good, I should bind and gag him. No, I'll leave him free to drive home. I doubt they'll nail him for aiding my flight from justice, since I didn't hurt anyone. It's a misdemeanor to fuel false reports, but he'll make up an alibi and the cops will drop the case because it's so embarrassing. Won't they?

Well in the end, we're all on our own.

In the airport rest room, I'll change into my light-brown, long-haired wig, tortoise-shell glasses, tennis shoes, and gray wool pantsuit. I'll leave with only the briefcase holding my laptop, old driver's license, and credit cards in my old name. He thinks I'm taking a plane, but in fact I'll shuttle to the bus station and catch a bus heading Houseward.

"You're getting rid of me, aren't you?"

"I like doing things myself. My family hasn't seen

me in eighteen years. Returning to Kansas won't be easy."

"Maybe you should call first," he says as if he didn't believe me.

"No," I answer sincerely; honesty's easier in the negative, and besides, his suggestion caught me off guard. "Definitely not."

There are times when the only way to escape from the past is to catch it off guard—abruptly stop fleeing, wheel around, chase it down. It's the same with all fears, even fear of death. Instead of running *before* death, one should try to run *after* death.

Okay, one should not try too hard.

I don't *really* want to catch up with my mother. I don't *really* want a showdown with death, or the past, but only some means to repeatedly return, back-and-forth, back-and-forth.

Imagine the rhythm of a swinging door.

Or the pendulum of a grandfather clock.

"*Hickory dickory dock! The mouse ran up the clock. The clock struck twelve, and down he fell. Hickory, dickory dock!*"

"That's not how it goes."

"Well that's how I remember it." I notice the tin remains on his lap. "Have some. Don't be squeamish." He snaps it shut.

By returning to The House, I seem to be returning

to my self, but it is not the same. (And never is.) I don't feel restored, but only perversely determined, and full of dread. Dread so intense, my limbs are numb.

Only a few more miles before I start over. "No wonder we're so tired." Exhausted. To stay alert, I tap SOSs against the steering wheel, while my right foot threatens to fall asleep on the gas pedal. My right foot feels very, very heavy. "Some things are out of my control."

The Bartender reopens the tin, bows his head. "Crackers," he observes, desultorily fingering the wig.

No, I cannot save my father or brother. They cannot save me.

So maybe I'm doing this to find out why I'm doing it.

Or because I think it's time to act, as if to get it over with — as if life *were* a series of fairy tales, and one could close this book, and open another. In choosing another, one might ask what the choices were. When I speak for "one," I imagine I speak for many.

The power of projection is enormous, of course. I'm repeating myself again. Oh sure, I wish I could stop — but then I don't.

A **WSP** n READING GROUP GUIDE

BYE-BYE
JANE RANSOM

ABOUT THIS GUIDE

The suggested questions are intended to
help your reading group find new and
interesting angles and topics for discussion
for Jane Ransom's *Bye-Bye.*
We hope that these ideas will enrich your
discussion and increase your enjoyment of
the book.

Many fine books from Washington Square
Press include Reading Group Guides. For a
complete listing, or to read the Guides
online, visit
http://www.simonsays.com/reading/guides

DISCUSSION QUESTIONS

1. The catalyst for the narrator's behavior seems to be the break-up of her marriage. What do you see as the reasons the marriage deteriorated?

2. We know the narrator's assumed name, Rose Anne Waldin. But we don't know her real name or the names of several other important characters in the book. What are they called? How does their "namelessness" shape the way we view them?

3. What is the narrator's new identity like? In what ways does it differ from her own?

4. The narrator is fascinated with the "Andorgenie." Why do you think this performance artist holds such an attraction for her?

5. Much of the novel focuses on the narrator's sexual adventures. What is her role with each of her lovers? What are her feelings about each one?

6. Although the narrator is very cynical about psychotherapy and psychoanalysis, she frequently analyzes her own behavior. What reasons does she give for acting as she does?

7. In talking about her family, the narrator tells a riddle, pointing out that she correctly answered it as a child. What is the riddle's relationship to the rest of the book? Is it symbolic of what is going on in the narrator's life?

8. What is the narrator's father like? Her brother? Why do you think she finally decides, after eighteen years, to go back home?

9. Why do you think the narrator's last lover is the bartender? Why do you think he is called The Bartender? Is his name symbolic? He is also a locksmith. Does this have a particular significance?

10. What or who is the narrator saying "bye-bye" to? Does she succeed? What do you think is going to happen to her?

AN INTERVIEW WITH THE AUTHOR:

Q: **You have published two other books, both poetry. What were the challenges you faced in writing a novel?**

A: First, I had to run away to Paris, away from anyone who knew me as a poet without a fiction track record. I didn't want to tell friends, "I'm writing a novel" and see the well-meaning skepticism in their faces. I'm hypersensitive to social interactions and struggle to maintain a writerly balance between arrogance and humility. Writing is a confidence trick. Writing is also an endurance test. I used to throw out half my poems even if I'd rewritten them a hundred times. One can't approach novel-writing with that sort of abandon. So it's a scary commitment. I started writing fiction because I'd begun reading more novels than poetry. My passion was shifting and I had to follow it. As the ancient Greeks wrote in the temple at Delphi: "Know thyself." That's my first tenet as a writer.

Q: **It is probably true that all creative writing is in some respects autobiographical. How much of your own life is in *Bye-Bye*?**

A: Often after a public reading, some stranger asks, "Aren't you being hard on your mother?" as if *Bye-Bye* were an autobiography. I take this as a compliment: I must have written convincing characters to leave readers thinking they're real. The protagonist Rosie may be my alter-ego, and I've given her bits of my own history, but I'd never take her drastic actions. Her mother, too, is mostly invented, inspired less by my mother than by filial emotions. I wanted, for example, to express a daughter's hopelessness of ever bring able to compete with Mom. So I made Rosie's mother intellectually foolproof, impossible to surmount. The two characters whom I lifted from life—virtually without elaboration—are the two who therefore seem most cartoonish and unbelievable: the father and brother. I probably should have fictionalized them more. But spending my adolescence with them did shape aspects of me which re-emerge in Rosie.

Q: **One reviewer said this was the "freshest writing about sex since Henry Miller." What in the way you write about sex makes it fresh? Do you, like Miller, have strong feelings about sex in our society and in art?**

A: "How dare you call me fresh!" Then I'd slap you, you'd slap me back, and we'd laugh at the beginnings of a possible slapstick sex act, replete with absurdity, wildly conflicting urges, and play. On my mother's side I'm descended from the Vaudeville Harrigans; sometimes I think of sexuality as a theater in which to enact one's various selves, including inner idiots and demons. Unfortunately, the real world often renders sex an all-too-serious issue. Men don't typically live in fear of sexual violence, nor suffer that inner split of virgin versus whore, so I suspect my concerns differ from Miller's. What we share is the conviction that sex can reveal much about the human condition. Miller made a heroic effort (and we can only ever try) to honestly express his personal vision of sexuality. Though they don't speak for me, I'm grateful to those male artists who thus expose themselves.

Q: What other writers influenced you while you were learning your craft?

A: Everything I read influences me, and I doubt I consciously know which writers I steal from most. When I began *Bye-Bye*, I was ensconced in the philosophies of Richard Rorty and Judith Butler. His pragmatism and her playfulness buoyed me intellectually, aesthetically, and emotionally. For me, Rorty and Butler permeate the novel, but I'm aware of only one reader who has picked up on this. As for fiction writers, I love so many: Thomas Bernhard, Flannery O'Connor, Jane Bowles, Nathalie Sarraute, Scott Bradfield's "The History of Luminous Motion" inspires me each time I reread it, as do the sentences of Tama Janowitz. I'm not attracted to overt plot as much as I am to the yumminess of language. And above all: rhythm. Rhythm is God.

Q: You've lived in many places in the world, yet you set your novel in New York. Why? Why not Paris?

A: New York epitomizes the threat and freedom of anonymity. I grew up in a small town in Indiana whose restrictive expectations I internalized and am still trying to escape. And I first moved to Manhattan after nearly four years in Puerto Rico, which Gabriel Garcia Marquez once called "an island surrounded by mirrors," trying to look out at the world, but only ever reflecting itself, blinded by provincialism. I've found such closed communities stifling. My first week in New York, I saw an apparently sane man wearing his bathrobe and slippers, shopping in a Korean grocery without causing a stir. This delighted me, and where else would it ever happen? Certainly not in oh-so-civilized Paris. My protagonist Rosie could thrive only in a city whose chaotic multiplicity creates plenty of spaces in which to act out.

Q: **This novel has won academic recognition and critical acclaim, but it took some persistence on your part to get it noticed. How did that happen? How strongly did you believe in the book?**

A: My first agent predicted *Bye-Bye* would snare a six-figure advance, but the megabucks publishers rejected it. "The best novel I've seen in years," said one editor, "but too dark for us to take the risk." Yet another called it "brilliant" but concluded it wasn't dark enough! Finally, the agent threw up her hands and told me, "Good luck." I sent the manuscript to whomever, wherever, until it won New York University's literary prize. In fact, that long wait turned out beneficial: When I returned to the novel to make final revisions, the passage of time had granted me invaluable perspective. Once I finish a book, I feel a stubborn parental loyalty to see it published. After it's out, however, we switch places: it becomes the parent, whom I must overthrow and whose wisdom I violently doubt. Eventually my hostility ebbs and the work again pleases me, although by then it's almost as if it had been written by someone else.